W9-APR-373

# Bozos on Patrol

Look for other books in the
Space Cadets series by R.L. Stine:

*Jerks-in-Training*
*Losers in Space*

# SPACE CADETS

**#3**

## Bozos on Patrol

### R.L. Stine

AN
**APPLE**
PAPERBACK

SCHOLASTIC INC.
New York Toronto London Auckland Sydney

If you purchased this book without a cover, you should be aware that this book is stolen property. It was reported as "unsold and destroyed" to the publisher, and neither the author nor the publisher has received any payment for this "stripped book."

No part of this publication may be reproduced in whole or in part, or stored in a retrieval system, or transmitted in any form or by any means, electronic, mechanical, photocopying, recording, or otherwise, without written permission of the publisher. For information regarding permission, write to Scholastic Inc., 730 Broadway, New York, NY 10003.

ISBN 0-590-44747-5

Copyright © 1992 by R.L. Stine. All rights reserved. Published by Scholastic Inc. APPLE PAPERBACKS is a registered trademark of Scholastic Inc.

12 11 10 9 8 7 6 5 4 3 2 1     2 3 4 5 6 7/9

Printed in the U.S.A.     28

First Scholastic printing, February 1992

# Bozos on Patrol

# 1

CADET BEEF HARDY, his wavy, blond hair shimmering under the bright ceiling lights, strode purposefully down the main hallway of the Space Academy. As he walked, taking regulation fourteen-inch strides, swinging his right arm at the regulation arc of forty-five degrees, Cadet Hardy thought about fertilizer.

He thought about fertilizer because he was on his way to see a big pile of it.

Just thinking about it filled him with pride.

This wasn't an ordinary pile of fertilizer, Hardy mused, his steel-gray eyes focused straight ahead, his boots clicking against the marble floor at a regulation twenty-two taps per minute. This pile of fertilizer was part of a top-secret operation. And Hardy was the only cadet who knew about it.

"Operation Spread It Around." That's what Space Academy Commander Donald Dorque had called it. Earlier that morning, Dorque had urgently summoned Hardy to his office.

"You wished to see me, Commander Dorque?" Hardy asked, giving a sharp, head-banging salute that sent him staggering back to the bookshelves against the wall.

"It's pronounced Dor*kay*," the headmaster replied. "Dor*kay*."

"Sorry, sir." Hardy regained his balance and stood at rigid attention, his head still throbbing. "You wished to see me, Commander Dor*kay*? Something about your daughter Debby? You'd like me to tutor her in wrestling, perhaps? I could be persuaded, sir."

"No, no." The Academy headmaster shook his bald head, his many chins bobbing from side to side. Although Dorque was quite short — four foot two, to be exact — standing straight and stiff in his uniform, he gave the appearance of someone nearly four feet tall.

For a little butterball of a man, the Commander was quite impressive, Hardy thought, staring at him. And he'd be even more impressive if he had remembered to remove the coat hanger from his jacket before putting it on that morning.

"Perhaps I could find a dark, romantic place somewhere under the stars tonight and tutor your daughter on the constellations, sir," Hardy suggested hopefully. "I could show her the difference between the Big Dipper and the Little Dipper. It's really quite fascinating."

"That's not what I had in mind," Dorque said sternly. He scratched his back, wondering why his uniform jacket felt so stiff that morning. "I wasn't thinking about my daughter. I was thinking about fertilizer."

"Fertilizer, sir?" Hardy couldn't hide his disappointment. He spent all of his time — when he wasn't studying the Space Academy Regulation Book — thinking about Debby Dorque, the Commander's beautiful, blonde-haired, blue-eyed daughter.

Hardy was nuts about her. She was an angel. An angel!

"Fertilizer," Commander Dorque repeated, bringing Hardy quickly back down to earth. "I'd like you to spread some."

Spread fertilizer? The idea didn't immediately appeal to Beef Hardy. In fact, he told himself, this assignment smells.

"Isn't this job better suited to the talents of the Space Cadets?" Hardy sniffed.

Commander Dorque shook his head. "I wouldn't trust those four idiots with fertilizer," he told Hardy.

The Commander, Hardy realized, was a lot smarter than he looked. There was no telling what the four irresponsible lunatics known as the Space Cadets might do if they got their hands on actual fertilizer.

"I guess I'm your man, sir," Hardy said, sending himself staggering once more into the book-shelves with a powerful, head-banging salute. "Perhaps your daughter would like to accompany me so that I might instruct her in the use of manual earth-moving tools?"

"Let's leave my daughter out of this, Hardy," the Commander whispered. "This is a top-secret fertilizer pile. I don't want anyone to get wind of it."

"I can keep a secret, sir," Hardy said solemnly. "What is the fertilizer to be used for?"

"That's a secret," Dorque confided.

"What is to be fertilized?"

"A secret," Dorque whispered.

"Well, where is the fertilizer?"

"That's a secret, too," Dorque revealed.

"And why is this such a big secret?" Hardy asked.

"The secret is a secret," Dorque told him. He raised a finger to his lips and went "*Shhhhh.*"

"The secret is a secret?" Hardy whispered.

"I can't answer that," Dorque said. "It's a se-cret."

"*What* is?" Hardy asked, completely confused.

"I can't tell you that, either," Dorque said.

"But what are we talking about?" Beef Hardy demanded.

"*Shhhh,*" Dorque repeated. "It's our little se-cret."

A few minutes later, Hardy marched out of

the headmaster's office, feeling proud and humble. His top-secret assignment was so top-secret that he really had no idea what it was. He knew only that he was to go out to the small patch of ground hidden to the left of the Rifle Practice Field, where he would find a big pile of top-secret fertilizer.

There, he would spread the fertilizer over the ground, and then water it thoroughly with a garden hose. Then he was to report back to the Commander on his progress. And, most important, no one — *no one* — was to know about it.

I'll probably win some sort of award or commendation for this, Hardy thought proudly as he headed toward the back exit of the Space Academy Tower. This assignment must have something to do with security, perhaps with the security of the entire Academy!

It must be some new kind of warning device, he figured. Or perhaps it's even some amazing new weapon that requires fertilizing and watering. Yes! Well, the Commander has certainly put this operation in good hands, Hardy congratulated himself.

He was nearly to the wide glass doorways that formed the back exit when Debby Dorque came lilting by. Beef stopped and gaped. She looked lovely. Her long blonde hair bobbed behind her like a wave of brilliant sunshine. Her blue eyes sparkled like a vibrant sky on a cloudless day.

Her chewing gum gleamed between her teeth.

He pulled himself up to attention and gave an impressive salute. "Hi, Debby," he said, flashing her his warmest, most adoring smile.

"Where are you headed?" she asked, eyeing him coldly.

"It's a secret," he confided, knowing it would impress her. "I can't tell you anything about it. I'm heading out on a top-secret operation." He paused, then dramatically added, "I — I don't know if I will ever return." He took a step back and waited for the admiration to show on her face.

"Oh, don't tell me Daddy has you watering his sweet potato patch!" she cried, tossing her head back in a burst of scornful laughter.

He watched her move down the hall, shaking her beautiful head and laughing uproariously.

Why doesn't she appreciate me? Beef wondered. Is it because I'm so superior to all the other cadets? Is it because I'm *too good*?

He picked up a shovel from the supply closet and headed out the door.

It was a blazing hot summer day. The sun reflected off the tall glass-and-steel Space Academy Tower as if it were a giant mirror. On the broad, grassy practice field that stretched behind the building and its immediate grounds, the twang of rifle fire could be heard. Cadets practicing their skills.

The small, muddy field with the fertilizer pile was easy to find. Hardy followed a swarm of buzzing flies directly to the secret spot. The pile was taller and smellier than he had imagined. He was already bathed in sweat by the time he reached it.

A single tree stood at the corner of the field, a garden hose coiled at the base, a fragile, low branch poking out from the trunk as if pointing to the fertilizer. Hardy reached both hands up to the branch and leaned his weight against it as he considered this difficult assignment.

Luckily, he spotted two plebes, looking hot and sun-drenched in their gold and gray uniforms, wandering off the rifle practice field. Feeling somewhat revived by their presence, Hardy called to them, waving them over.

The two young, red-faced trainees loped quickly up to Hardy, stopping at the edge of the field to salute. Without warning, Hardy shot out his right fist, catching the shorter plebe in the mouth.

The plebe cried out. Blood began to roll down his chin. "Why did you do that, sir?" he asked weakly, still stunned.

"Just straightening my shirt cuff," Hardy said. He shot out his left fist, giving the other plebe a hard smack in the eye. "There. I think these cuffs are straight now," he said, examining both sleeves. Having shown these two young men who was boss, he proceeded to confide in them. "I have a nice assignment for you two plebes."

As the trainees held their bleeding faces in their hands, Hardy ordered them to spread the fertilizer over the muddy field. "But — but there's only one shovel," the plebe with the swelling eye protested.

Hardy shook his head. "No. *I'm* using the shovel. I'm *leaning* on it," he told them. "You boys will have to use your hands."

All of the color seemed to drain from their swollen faces. They glanced at each other, then at the tall heap of fly-covered fertilizer. Realizing they had no choice but to obey a superior's order, they silently rolled up their sleeves and dug in.

Standing in the shade of the small tree, leaning on the shovel, Hardy enjoyed watching them work. Supervising a job like this can be pretty tough, he thought. But I know I can handle it.

The sun rose higher in the sky, and the day grew even hotter. Soon, there was only a small patch of shade for Hardy to stay comfortable in as he supervised. Constantly swatting at the swarming flies, the two plebes worked diligently, carrying handfuls of the loamy fertilizer, spreading it thickly over the muddy field, taking deep breaths and then holding it because of the pungent aroma.

Three hours later, the ground was covered. The fertilizer pile had shrunk until it was less than three feet deep. The plebes' uniforms were soiled and decidedly fragrant. Bathed in sweat, the two young men stopped to catch their breath.

"Okay," Hardy called cheerfully. "Nice work. You two can turn yourselves in now for disciplinary action."

"Huh?" Their faces still swollen, they both gaped at him in astonishment.

"I'm really sorry," Hardy said sympathetically. "But you rolled up your sleeves. That's a violation of the Dress Code. You'll have to go on report. I personally would overlook it, but we're all on the Honor Code, right? The Honor Code leaves me no choice. Go turn yourselves in right now. Perhaps they'll be lenient, and you'll only be suspended for six months."

Shading his eyes from the sun, Hardy watched the two plebes slump unhappily back to the Academy building. Then, humming brightly to himself, he picked up the nozzle of the garden hose, turned it on, and began to water the newly fertilized field.

An excellent job, if I don't say so myself, he thought.

He wondered what kind of reward he would receive for his hard work.

He was thinking about his reward, dreamily allowing his eyes to follow the sparking spray of the water, when Commander Dorque popped up at his side.

Startled out of his daydreams, Beef Hardy cried out and lowered the garden hose, sending a rushing torrent of water into the Commander's face.

"Turn it off! Turn it off!" Dorque sputtered, trying unsuccessfully to dodge out of the way of the powerful stream.

The nozzle seemed to be stuck. It took Hardy a while to stop the flow of water. Finally, he figured out that he could aim the hose *away* from Commander Dorque. He did so, then managed to shut it off.

"There. That's better," Hardy said, smiling triumphantly. "Too bad you didn't bring a towel, sir." He chuckled, trying to keep things light.

Commander Dorque shook his entire body. He looked like a fat bulldog trying to dry himself after a bath. "Hardy — "

"The ground is fertilized and watered, sir," Hardy offered proudly. "Mission accomplished."

Commander Dorque squeezed the front of his uniform jacket between his hands. Water poured out onto the ground. "Good work, Hardy," he said, his beady little eyes surveying the field. "But forget about this operation. I've got a bigger problem right now."

"The Space Cadets!" Hardy guessed. "What have they done, sir?"

"It's not what they've done," the Commander replied, sighing wearily. "It's what they *could* do."

He squeezed some more water from his jacket, then leaned forward to confide in Hardy. "There's a camera crew here," he said, lowering his voice even though no one was around.

"Making a movie?" Hardy asked, slapping a fly on top of the Commander's bald head. "Got him!"

"They're from Space Patrol Headquarters. They're making a film, a documentary, about the Space Academy. My superior officer, General Innis Outt, sent them here. They just arrived and already they're climbing all over the place, filming everything. The film is supposed to show real life at the Academy. It's a public relations thing, I guess. What a nuisance!"

Hardy reached down and slapped at another fly on the Commander's round, pink head. This time he missed.

"Hardy, may I ask why you're doing that?" Dorque asked irritably.

"I hate flies," Hardy told him.

"Those four idiots are going to embarrass me in this film. I just know it," Commander Dorque continued earnestly. "This film is going to be shown all over the galaxy. I don't want to look like a fool in it. I don't want to see their grinning faces in it. I don't want them to embarrass me."

"Well," said Hardy thoughtfully, "perhaps your daughter Debby and I could get together tonight and think of some ways to — "

"Forget about my daughter!" the Commander bellowed. "You know that Debby is completely infatuated with the Space Cadets' leader, Hunk, or Punk, or Junk — whatever his name is."

"It's Hunk," Hardy said through gritted teeth. What did Debby see in Hunk, anyway? Hunk couldn't recite all three thousand Academy regulations the way Beef could. No way! Hunk couldn't even recite the alphabet without having to look up some of the letters in the dictionary!

"I want you to make sure that the Space Cadets don't appear in this film," Dorque said. "I don't care what you do, Hardy. Just keep them from embarrassing me in this film. Keep them out of it! Understand?"

"Yes, sir. It will be a pleasure, sir." Beef started to give one of his impressive but deadly salutes, but caught himself just in time.

They both turned back toward the Space Academy Building. And both uttered cries of surprise when they saw the camera crew — two men with cameras, and a woman trailing with a microphone and tape recorder — hurrying across the Rifle Practice Field toward them.

"No!" Dorque cried in alarm. "I don't want them here!" He started gesturing and shouting at them, "Go back! Go back!"

Then, as Hardy watched in alarm, Commander Dorque began to run toward the three equipment-laden invaders, still motioning with his hands for them to stay away.

The pudgy Commander had run about four steps when the coat hanger in the back of his jacket caught on the low tree branch.

"Whoa!!"

Hooked by the branch, Commander Dorque spun up into the air. For a brief moment, it looked as if the slender branch would hold him. But then it cracked and broke. With a howl, Dorque toppled face down into the three-foot-deep pile of fertilizer.

When he managed to pull himself up, covered from head to foot in a thick, loamy layer of brown gook, and began to wipe the fertilizer away from his eyes with both hands, the camera crew was there, their cameras whirring away.

"Candid moment! A candid moment!" the woman with the sound equipment was chanting gleefully. "Use your zoom!"

As the Commander stood helplessly in the muck with the cameras whirring, Beef Hardy carefully straightened the cuffs on his shirtsleeves and tightened his tie. A lot of people would be seeing this film. Hardy wanted to make sure that he followed the dress code to a T.

# 2

"HEY — WHERE'D EVERYBODY GO?" Shaky asked, his eyes nervously searching the nearly deserted mess hall.

"Yo, man — who cares?" Hunk replied impatiently. "Pay attention to your drooling."

At their corner table, the four Space Cadets were engaging in one of their most challenging sports activities — a drooling contest. Which explained why the normally jam-packed mess hall was nearly deserted at lunchtime.

No one — not even the most insensitive, iron-stomached cadet — liked to sit and watch four young men drip gobs of drool from their open mouths. So whenever the four friends began to warm up for another hotly contested drooling match, chairs scraped against the linoleum floor, lunches were abandoned, and the room cleared out as quickly as if someone had set off a stink bomb (another popular Space Cadets sport).

14

"Here goes a golden gobber," proclaimed Rip. Rip weighed three hundred pounds. He got his nickname from the sound his uniform trousers made whenever he bent over. He claimed that his weight was a real advantage in this sport, allowing him the ballast required for truly major-league drools.

Hunk, the wavy dark brown-haired, broad-chested, handsome leader of the group, claimed that his height advantage made him a champion, allowing him to suspend the drool in midair for greater lengths of time. Statistically, Hunk was a superior drooler, although his jutting chin often got in the way.

Shaky, the skinny, needle-shaped member of the Space Cadets, tried hard and drooled with true intensity. But he was too nervous to be a real champion. He had difficulty holding his head in position, the results being that the front of his shirt usually ended up sticky and sopping wet.

Andy, the fourth Space Cadet, was an android. This was a well-kept secret that only his three companions knew. Androids were not allowed in the Space Academy.

It was a constant struggle to keep anyone from finding out that Andy wasn't human. Even his participation in the lunchtime drooling contests put Andy at risk — mainly because he drooled 4-in-1 oil instead of saliva, and instead of dripping to the floor, it often shot across the room.

"Oh, space spit!" Shaky exclaimed angrily as another gob dripped down the front of his shirt.

Andy beeped and laughed. He was standing in a puddle of oil.

All four Space Cadets stood with their backs to the table, tilting their heads slightly as they drooled. "Will someone close that window?" Shaky cried shrilly. "The wind keeps blowing it back in my face!"

"You've got to think about wind velocity," Rip instructed him. "That's part of the skill." He sent a large gob dribbling down to his black shoes. "Oops. I'm out."

The object of the sport was to keep the drool suspended from your mouth longer than any other player. If it hit the floor, you were out.

This made for exciting — and lengthy — contests. And while the rules were quite simple, it still could be a challenging and dangerous sport. Once, for example, Shaky received a severe tongue sprain. And during that same contest, Andy ran low on oil and had to be rushed to the shop for an emergency lube job.

Despite the physical dangers, it was such an exciting and competitive sport that Hunk had considered writing to the Olympic Committee to get drooling accepted as an Olympic event. But he never wrote the letter, mainly because he couldn't spell *Olympic* or *Committee,* and he really wasn't sure how many u's there were in *drooling*.

16

Of course, there were other problems. While drooling matches were a terrific participation sport, they weren't much of a spectator sport, as the nearly empty mess hall demonstrated. This didn't discourage the four friends, who took their sports seriously. It was important for future Interplanetary Space Patrolmen to stay in shape, after all.

"Yo, Andy, stick out your tongue further," Hunk instructed. "You're not getting the right velocity-downdraft ratio."

Andy stuck his tongue out a bit further, allowing the thick, viscous oil to run down his chin.

"No. Stick it out further," Hunk urged.

Andy stuck the tongue out another quarter-inch.

"Further," Hunk insisted.

Andy stuck his tongue out further, and it fell out, plopping onto the floor.

"Oh, how gross!" Shaky cried, his chin covered in drool. He covered his eyes with his hands.

"Waawaaa wah wah waaaawa," Andy said.

"Huh?" Hunk replied. It was usually hard to understand Andy. But it was even harder to understand him without a tongue.

Andy picked up the pink, floppy tongue and popped it back in his mouth.

"Yuck," Shaky said, still hiding his eyes.

"No problem," Andy told them, smiling. "No problem. It's a clip-on."

"Okay — let's go again," Rip urged. "Round thirty-four! Ready?"

"No!" Shaky cried. "Dry Mouth! Dry Mouth! Time out!"

Dry Mouth was a serious hazard in this sport. Shaky made a desperate run for the water fountain across the room.

When he returned, he was surprised to see that Debby Dorque had appeared in the mess hall and was talking animatedly to Hunk.

"Where *were* you?" Debby was demanding.

"Uh . . . we were here," Hunk told her, looking to his buddies for support. Then he flashed her his 352-tooth smile, the smile he knew she couldn't resist.

Debby resisted it this time. "You were here in the lunch room all this time?" she cried, her voice almost so high that only dogs could hear it.

"Yeah . . . we were drooling," Rip told her with no little pride. "I did a double dribbler with a spin. You should've seen it!"

Debby Dorque rolled her eyes. She glared at Hunk. "You were in here drooling while the rest of us were taking the Galactic Geometry exam?"

Hunk slapped his broad, handsome forehead. "The exam! Wow! I forgot all about it."

Andy, who had a bad habit of copying nearly everything his buddies did, slapped his forehead, too. He must have slapped it a little too hard because his tongue popped out again and flew up in the air.

Luckily, Rip caught it in midair before Debby saw what it was. He stuffed it quickly into his trouser pocket.

"Waah wawa wawa wah!" Andy declared.

"What's wrong with him?" Debby asked Hunk.

"Oh, he's just upset about missing the exam," Hunk replied, thinking quickly.

"Wah wah," Andy said.

"Well, you should *all* be upset," Debby scolded. "You're all going to flunk Galactic Geometry now."

Debby didn't enjoy scolding Hunk. He was her dream man, after all. Her cuddly cadet. Her handsome hero. She was almost as crazy about him as *he* was!

So why did he have to be so irresponsible?

"Hey — flunking Galactic Geometry is no big deal," Hunk assured her.

"How come?" she asked.

"Because we're flunking all our other courses, too!" Hunk exclaimed.

"Right!" Rip agreed, slapping Hunk on the back.

"Wah wah!" Andy declared and slapped Shaky on the back.

Then Shaky slapped Hunk, Rip slapped Andy, Andy slapped Rip, and Rip slapped Hunk again.

"I'm glad you guys take this seriously," Debby said sarcastically. And then her face crumpled into sadness. "Oh, Hunk," she cried, "you're going to flunk out, and I'll never see you again."

"Huh? Flunk out?" Hunk looked stunned. The thought had never occurred to him.

"You mean if we flunk all our courses, we'll have to leave?" Rip asked, suddenly concerned.

"We're doomed! Doomed!" Shaky cried, his eyes wide with fear, his bony hands pulling at his oily, blond hair.

"Wah wahwah waaah," Andy added with equal fervor.

"There's nothing Daddy would like better than to see all four of you pack your bags and leave in disgrace," Debby said sadly.

"Couldn't we leave in a taxi?" Hunk asked.

"Daddy will dance on his desk. He'll throw a party on the day you flunk out," Debby continued.

"Hey — will there be food at the party?" Rip asked. He hadn't eaten for nearly an hour, and his stomach was starting to gnaw and growl.

"You won't be invited," Debby told him harshly.

"We're doomed! Doomed!" Shaky repeated, passionately tearing out a hunk of his hair.

"Wah wah wah!" Andy cried and, copying Shaky, he reached up and yanked out a hunk of his hair, removing a large chunk of his scalp with it.

"There must be something we can do," Hunk said, realizing the gravity of the situation. He gazed deeply into Debby's clear blue eyes, trying to see his reflection in them, wondering if his hair was mussed.

"Well . . ." Debby replied thoughtfully, "maybe you could do something for extra credit?"

"We don't have any credit at all!" Shaky wailed, shaking his narrow, pencillike head. "Any credit we'd get would be extra!"

"You mean like, do a project or something?" Hunk asked her, ignoring Shaky's miserable wails.

"Yeah," Debby said, smiling as she became more enthusiastic about the idea. "If you do a special project — something really impressive, something that will show you really deserve extra credit — then there's no way Daddy will be able to flunk you!"

"And we can go to the party?" Rip asked eagerly.

Debby ignored him, staring happily at Hunk. "You just have to think of a really good extra-credit project, and then you guys have to do a super job on it."

"Yo, well, that should be easy," Hunk said, giving her his warmest, most reassuring smile, the one he knew drove her absolutely wild.

"Maybe we could use our drooling talents in our extra-credit project," Rip suggested. "That could be impressive."

"Yeah!" Hunk agreed, slapping Rip on the back.

Then Rip slapped Hunk on the back, Andy slapped Rip, Shaky slapped Andy, and Andy slapped himself.

"I think you'd better give it some more thought," Debby told them. "Your entire careers depend on it, after all. You *do* want to be in the Interplanetary Space Patrol, don't you?"

"Yeah!" the four Space Cadets quickly replied.

"In the Space Patrol, they serve a hot lunch every day," Rip added enthusiastically. "And unlimited snacks."

"I've got to run. But I'm counting on you to come up with a really terrific project," Debby said, flashing Hunk a warm smile before hurrying out of the room.

They watched her leave. Then Rip handed Andy back his tongue, which was only slightly wrinkled from being in Rip's pocket, and they resumed their match.

"I believe it's your drool," Hunk told Shaky.

Shaky took a deep breath and let fly.

They were still competing half an hour later when the camera crew wandered in, lugging their equipment. Seeing this interesting and unusual competition in progress, the cameras were set up, the microphone put in place, and the event was recorded on film for all to see.

"Why are you cadets drooling like that?" the woman holding the microphone asked.

"Because we like to roller-skate," Hunk told her, wiping his chin with the back of his hand.

She looked confused. "I'm confused," she said.

"We like to roller-skate," Hunk explained. "But there's no skating rink at the Academy."

"Yeah. We need a rink," Rip added. "We tried skating in the halls, but we kept falling down the stairs."

"So we do this instead," Hunk continued.

"Oh. That makes sense," the woman said, glancing at her two companions, rolling her eyes. "Well, just go on the way you were. Pretend that we're not here."

As the cameras began to whir again, the four Space Cadets resumed their drooling positions.

"Hey — we're going to be movie stars!" Rip declared, up to his ankles in a puddle of drool.

Hunk turned so the camera could capture his good side.

"Just act natural," instructed the woman holding the microphone.

"We are," Hunk said, the drool running slowly, majestically, down his perfect chin.

# 3

COMMANDER DORQUE TILTED back his big, leather desk chair and took a bite of his sandwich. He enjoyed having lunch alone in the quiet privacy of his office. It gave him time to think.

And he had a lot to think about.

For one thing, he had to think about his sandwich. Why was it so dry? Chewing hard, his many chins wobbling as he chewed, he examined it. It seemed to be a pocket made of some sort of leathery dough. He couldn't tell what the filling was. But whatever it was, it was much too dry.

He took another bite, then pushed a button on his intercom to talk to his secretary in the outer office. "Miss Moon, would you please get me a cup of coffee from the vending machine?"

There was a brief silence on the other end. Then Miss Moon spoke up in a quivering voice. "How do you take your coffee, sir?"

"In a cup," Dorque replied.

"Cream or milk?" Miss Moon asked from the other room.

"Yes," Dorque told her.

"Sugar?"

"Yes, please," said Dorque impatiently.

"Regular coffee or decaf?" Miss Moon asked.

"Regular coffee," was the Commander's reply.

"Colombian or Italian roast?"

"Italian will be fine," Dorque said, tapping his stubby fingers restlessly on his desktop.

"Italian espresso or regular blend?" Miss Moon queried.

"Regular blend!" Dorque screamed.

"Brewed or percolated?"

"I don't care!" Commander Dorque screamed, bobbing up and down on the chair like a bouncing beach ball.

"Drip grind or all-purpose grind?"

"Huh?"

"Please make up your mind, sir!" Miss Moon demanded.

"Drip. I'll take the drip," he snarled.

"And was that one sugar or two?"

"One! Just one!" He slapped his forehead. He realized he was hyperventilating.

"You did say milk, didn't you?"

"Yes! Yes! Yes!" Dorque was standing on his chair now, screaming at the top of his lungs.

"Well, I'm sorry, sir." Miss Moon spoke reluctantly through the intercom.

"Sorry?"

"I don't know how to work the coffee machine."

"Huh?" The Commander's voice broke. He slid, defeated, back into the chair. "You don't?"

"You *know* I have no skills, sir," Miss Moon scolded. Her voice was shrill. She was about to start crying. "You *know* I can't do anything. I have no training. I have no ability whatsoever. You *know* that, Commander."

"Yes, I do," Dorque admitted guiltily.

"So why do you rub it in? Why are you constantly reminding me of how worthless I am as a secretary?"

The Commander swallowed a hunk of the dry sandwich. "I'm terribly sorry," he managed to say, chewing hard. "I don't mean to be cruel, Miss Moon."

He could hear her sniffling on the other end.

"Miss Moon, why don't you take the rest of the afternoon off?" he suggested.

"Thank you, sir. I will." She sniffled some more. "And, sir? About that raise I asked you for . . ."

"Yes. Okay," the Commander quickly agreed. *Anything* to cheer her up! "You may have the extra thousand dollars a month."

"Oh, thank you, sir," she replied gratefully. "That really makes me feel appreciated."

I'd appreciate a cup of coffee, the headmaster thought bitterly, choking down another chunk of sandwich.

"One more thing before I leave," Miss Moon's voice shrilled over the intercom.

"Yes, Miss Moon?"

"Have you by any chance seen my change purse anywhere?"

"Change purse?"

"Yes. It's a white plastic change purse. I know I had it with me this morning."

Commander Dorque looked down at the object in his hand. He gulped and dropped it onto the desk. Feeling a bit queasy, he leaned into the intercom. "I believe I've just eaten most of your change purse, Miss Moon."

"That really wasn't necessary, sir," she scolded. "There's a perfectly good sandwich waiting for you on the table across from your desk."

He apologized for a few minutes, feeling somewhat bloated. It was a relief to hear the office door close behind her. He sat quietly for a few moments, and then suddenly remembered his secret gardening project.

It was fertilized and watered, but there was still work to be done. A lot of nurturing. A lot of tender loving care.

And then in a few months, thought the Commander dreamily, his sweet potato crop would be ripe. Ready to take to Carmella Flan, the Academy cook, to be turned into sweet potato pudding, his all-time favorite.

Mine, all mine! he thought hungrily, tossing

the chewed-up plastic change purse across the room.

And these weren't ordinary sweet potatoes that he had planted so secretly on that hidden field. They were prize sweet potatoes from the Yam II Galaxy, the softest, sweetest, *kindest* sweet potatoes in the universe!

Something to live for, Dorque thought. Something to *die* for!

But now the field needed to be hoed, the newly fertilized ground softened up. He decided to do it himself. He'd use one of those new turbo-powered, drive-around hoes the Academy had purchased.

His fingers trembling with excitement, he dialed the number of the Academy Grounds Administrator. A man's voice answered after the first ring. "Hello?"

"Who's speaking?" the Commander asked.

"Yes," the man replied.

"Who?"

"Yes. Hu," the man said.

"I'd like to know who's speaking," Commander Dorque repeated impatiently.

"Yes. Hu's speaking," came the reply.

"Would you *please* stop repeating that like a parrot and tell me who's speaking?" Dorque bellowed.

"Yes. Hu's speaking. This is Hu."

"Who?"

"Yes."

"Oh. Hu." Commander Dorque mopped his brow with a linen handkerchief. "Right. Of course. Hi, Hu."

"Hi," said Hu.

"This is the headmaster speaking, Hu."

"Oh. Hi, Commander Dorque."

"It's Dor*kay*," the Commander corrected. "It's pronounced Dor*kay*."

"Sorry," said Hu, snickering for some reason. "How may I help you today?"

"How, Hu?"

"Yes, how?"

"Well, I need a hoe."

"A hoe?" Hu asked.

"Yes. I thought I'd do some hoeing. You know. Get a little exercise. Get close to the soil." The Commander didn't want the Grounds Administrator to know he'd planted a secret field of sweet potatoes. He didn't want *anyone* to know. He wanted them all for himself.

"What kind of hoe would you like, Commander?" Hu asked.

"What's available, Hu?"

"Well," said Hu thoughtfully, "let me see . . . I've got a slow hoe, a low hoe, a high hoe, a tow hoe, and a hoe hoe."

"A hoe hoe?"

"Ho ho to you, too, sir. You're certainly in a good mood today."

Commander Dorque could hear the man chuckling on the other end of the line. What's so darned funny? he wondered.

"Which do you recommend, Hu?" Dorque asked.

"Well, the low hoe is faster than the slow hoe. The high hoe cuts deeper than the low hoe. And the tow hoe is more efficient than the high hoe."

"What about the hoe hoe?" Dorque asked.

"The hoe hoe? It's so-so."

The Commander mopped his furrowed brow. "So?"

"Sorry, sir. The sow hoe is no go. It's broken. I believe we have a blow hoe."

"Hu, how does the blow hoe work?" Dorque asked, his beady eyes rolling about in his head.

"First it hoes it, then it blows it. So? Want to give the hoe a go?"

"I don't know," Dorque said. He glanced down at his desk calendar, and his eyes bulged as he realized he was late for a very important appointment. "I'll have to call you back," he said, standing up.

"A back hoe? Yes, we have a back hoe," Hu told him.

"No, I have to go!" Dorque insisted.

"Goh? It's Goh's day off," Hu said. "Besides, Goh doesn't do hoes. Only Hu has hoes."

"Who?"

"Right."

Commander Dorque slammed down the receiver. He'd have to straighten out this hoe business later. Right now, he was late for a very important reception. Miss Moon should have reminded him of it, but of course, she didn't know how to read his calendar.

He tightened his tie and buttoned his uniform jacket. Then, checking in the mirror by the office door to make sure there wasn't anything hanging out of his nose, he hurried to the main hall.

Already gathered in the front lobby were several Space Academy officers and a smiling group of officials from the planet Schnauzer. The Schnauzers, as they liked to be called, had come with a present, which they were about to unveil.

Funny. They don't look like Schnauzers, Commander Dorque thought as he hurried to the front of the lobby to greet his guests. They looked more like armadillos, the Commander thought, staring at their hard, layered, plated skin and sharp, pointed, single horns that jutted out from the center of their heads.

They were about the same height as Commander Dorque, and just as round and pudgy. Their uniforms consisted of two tiny, tight bands of bright red cloth, worn like bikinis across their bulging tops and bottoms.

After apologizing to the visitors, the headmaster took his place in the front of the audience of officers. The camera crew was off to one side, he

31

noticed, their cameras whirring away.

Well, this will look impressive in the film, Dorque thought happily. He wondered if Cadet Hardy was accomplishing his assignment, keeping the four Space Cadets out of the film.

One of the Schnauzers lumbered up beside a large rectangular object that was draped in canvas and began the presentation.

The Space Academy was being given some kind of mural, the Commander learned. "As a symbol of friendship between this Academy and our own Academy," announced the beaming Schnauzer in a booming deep voice, "we are lending you for one year our most priceless work of art."

The Schnauzer tugged a rope and the canvas fell away, revealing an enormous mural, filled from top to bottom with what appeared to be ancient scrawls and cave drawings.

"These drawings are five thousand years old," the Schnauzer announced with pride. "This is the oldest work of art remaining from the early days of our planet. Its value cannot be measured. It will hang here in your main hall for one year, as a demonstration of the great regard we Schnauzers have for your planet and for this Academy."

The large hall rang out with applause. Then everyone stood admiring the wondrous work of art, the ancient drawings and symbols, the intricate markings painted so many centuries ago.

Commander Dorque, a thoughtful look on his face, stepped forward to accept the gift. If only I had known this presentation was today, I could have prepared a proper speech, he was thinking as he once again shook hands with the members of the Schnauzer delegation.

Oh, well. I think I can ad-lib something to convey my gratitude to these generous creatures.

The Commander stepped up to the microphone and cleared his throat. "Gee, thanks," he said.

# 4

IN THEIR DORM ROOM high in the Space Academy Tower, the four Space Cadets were thinking hard, trying to decide what they could do to earn the extra credit that would keep them from flunking out.

"Hmmmm." Shaky nervously paced back and forth, wringing his bony hands. Rip chewed thoughtfully on a chocolate bar. Hunk stared out the window, admiring his reflection in the glass, wondering if he'd look even more perfect if he parted his hair on *both* sides. Andy, performing a self-test on his diodes and transistors, beeped softly in the corner.

"Hmmm," Shaky repeated. "Extra credit. . . . What could we do?" He snapped his fingers. "Maybe we could write something. You know. A report about something."

"A report about what?" Hunk asked glumly.

Shaky shrugged his narrow shoulders. "Maybe

a report about how we'd like extra credit?"

"I know!" Andy spoke up brightly. "How about a report on dysfunctionalism in the bilevel lateral-motion drives in subcompact android forms?"

Rip burped loudly in Andy's direction. "How about a report on *that*?" he grumbled.

"I like my idea better," Andy insisted.

Rip burped again. He could never burp just once.

"Yo. We can't write a report for extra credit," Hunk said, turning away from the window. "We aren't any good at writing reports. If we write a report, it'll be terrible, and we'll only flunk *worse*!"

"Hunk is right," Rip agreed, reaching for another candy bar and biting right through the paper. "No report."

"I know!" cried Andy. "Let's build a model of an android!"

The other three ignored him. They thought silently for a long while.

"Yo — let's do a project!" Hunk suggested finally.

"A project! Yeah!" Rip agreed.

"What's a project?" Andy asked.

"What kind of project?" Shaky asked Hunk.

"Hey — I thought of the hard part. Now it's *your* turn to think of something!" Hunk declared, crossing his arms over his chest.

"We can't do a project," Rip said, stuffing the

entire candy bar in his mouth sideways.

"Rip is right," Andy agreed. "Because we don't know what a project is."

"Well, if we don't do a report and we don't do a project, what can we do?" Shaky asked shrilly, biting his nails as he paced.

"Let's go for a walk," Hunk said.

Shaky stopped in his tracks. "Huh? Can we get extra credit for *that*?"

"No. I *mean* let's go for a walk," Hunk repeated. "Maybe it'll give us some ideas."

Thinking hard, the four friends slipped out the door and headed toward the elevators.


With her mane of flowing red hair and her sparkling emerald-green eyes, Camembert (Cammy) Cheesewell was the most beautiful of all the female cadets. She was also the most sought after by the male cadets.

But Cammy had eyes for only one cadet. And here he was, standing beside her in the library right now. Sighing, she stared into Beef Hardy's steel-gray eyes and blushed.

Beef was also red-faced. Just before Cammy had arrived, he was tucking his uniform shirt into his trousers, and a shirt flap had become stuck in the zipper. Before he could do anything about it, Cammy had come in. Beef blushed because he knew he was out of uniform and was violating Dress Code Regulation 402–W, which was very specific about shirt flaps caught in zippers.

The Academy library was a wonderfully comfortable, quiet room that looked like someone's den. It had luxurious blue carpeting on the floor. Dark, Victorian-looking oil paintings covered one wall. The floor-to-ceiling bookshelves were made of the finest oak and mahogany. In addition to long, handsomely crafted oak study tables, there were old-fashioned-looking, high-backed, over-stuffed armchairs to sit in.

Walking bent over with his legs tightly together so that Cammy couldn't see the shirt flap poking out of his fly, Hardy led her to two facing armchairs and motioned solemnly for her to sit down.

"Beef — I'm so shocked!" Cammy cried.

Beef's face turned purple. "It just got stuck! I couldn't help it!" he blurted out.

Her face filled with confusion. "I'm so shocked that you asked me out on a study date," she said, finishing her thought. "I — I didn't think you were . . . uh . . . interested in me. I mean . . ."

Hardy breathed a sigh of relief. What is she *talking* about? he wondered. He quickly grabbed a magazine off the table beside him and placed it over his lap.

He wished it were Debby Dorque sitting across from him now, helping him to plot against the

Space Cadets. But Debby would never help him. She was too crazy about that punk Hunk. And so he had been forced to enlist Cammy's aid. She had helped him before in battles against those four losers.

But what was all this talk about a study date? And why was she staring into his eyes like that? Maybe she's nearsighted, he decided.

He hoped that wasn't true. Being nearsighted was a violation of Personal Health Rule 123–RD. He'd have to turn her in.

"I need your help, Cadet Cheesewell," he said, balancing the magazine on his lap and leaning toward her confidentially.

"What can I do for you?" she asked eagerly. "Can I fluff up that chair cushion for you? Can I open a window? Or close one? Can I hold that magazine for you while you read it?"

"No! No! Don't hold the magazine!" Hardy cried in horror, holding it down with both hands.

"Just trying to be helpful," Cammy said, flashing him a warm smile.

"No. I need your help in a top-secret mission," Hardy explained, lowering his voice again.

Cammy beamed, her eyes sparkling like twin emeralds. "I *love* top-secret missions!" she gushed.

"Ssshhhh," Hardy warned. "The walls have ears."

They both looked up at the wallpaper, which

featured a vertical pattern of red and blue ears against a background of gray.

"I've written our mission down on a slip of paper," Hardy whispered, reaching into his uniform jacket pocket. He pulled out a slip of paper and handed it to Cammy. "Here. Be sure to eat it so no one else can read it."

Cammy eagerly took the slip of paper from him and jammed it into her mouth. She chewed twice and then swallowed it.

"Uh . . . one slight problem," Hardy whispered.

"What's that, Beef?"

"You were supposed to *read* it first!"

"Oh," Cammy replied, blushing prettily. She tried coughing up the paper, but it was too late. "Does this mean the mission is scrubbed?" she asked.

Cadet Hardy shook his head. "No problem," he whispered. "I also wrote the purpose of our mission down in this loose-leaf notebook." He pulled out a blue loose-leaf notebook from behind the chair cushion and handed it to Cammy.

She took it from him, raised it to her mouth, and began to chew on it.

"Whoa. Hold on. You don't have to eat the loose-leaf notebook," Beef said, pulling it away just in time.

Cammy looked very relieved.

She opened the cover and began to read the first page. It read:

1. Stop chewing my toenails.
2. Stop sniffing my armpits when no one is looking.

Cammy's face filled with surprise. She held the page up to Beef. "Is *this* our mission?"

Cadet Hardy's mouth dropped open in embarrassment. "No. Those are my personal goals for this year. Turn the page, Cadet Cheesewell."

Cammy turned to the next sheet in the notebook. It read:

## TOP-SECRET MISSION:
## KEEP THE SPACE CADETS OUT OF THE DOCUMENTARY FILM

Then, down at the bottom of the lined sheet of paper, printed in smaller letters, were the words:

(Possible solution: Kill them??)

Cammy slammed the notebook shut and handed it back to Hardy. "This is a difficult mission, Beef," she whispered, her eyes darting to the door to make sure they weren't being overheard.

"The filmmakers are everywhere," Hardy replied. "But I promised Commander Dorque that I'd keep those four troublemakers out of the

40

film — even if it meant breaking a few regulations."

Cammy felt a tingle run down her spine. She loved it when Beef talked about breaking regulations.

"How are we going to do it?" she asked. "Do you have a P-O-O?"

"A *what*?" Hardy cried.

"Do you have a P-O-O?" Cammy repeated, whispering.

Hardy thought hard about it. Finally, he was forced to ask, "What's a P-O-O?"

"Plan Of Operation," Cammy replied.

"Oh," Hardy said. He snickered. "You mean an M-O-O. Do I have an M-O-O."

"Huh? A cow?" Cammy asked, confused.

"No. Method Of Operation," Hardy informed her.

"No," she said, tossing her coppery hair behind her shoulders. "I mean, do you have a W-T-K-T-S-C-O-O-T-F?"

"I'd better go get my Academy Code Book," Hardy said thoughtfully. "What exactly is a W-T-K-T-S-C-O-O-T-F?"

"Way To Keep The Space Cadets Out Of The Film," Cammy told him, marking off each word on her fingers.

"N-O," Hardy replied.

"What?" she asked. "N-O? I don't understand. Is that in the code book?"

"Maybe we'd better stop using letters," Hardy suggested. "I don't have a plan — yet. But that's why I suggested we meet in the library. There *must* be a good idea in one of these books." He gestured to the entire wall of books beside them.

"How about in that book up there?" Cammy pointed to a large, leatherbound volume high above their heads on the top shelf.

"What's it called?" Hardy asked, impressed with Cammy's eyesight. She wasn't nearsighted after all. What a relief. That meant he wouldn't have to report her.

Cammy squinted to read the title. "It's called *The Boys' and Girls' First Book of Evil Plans*," she reported.

"Yes!" Hardy cried enthusiastically. "That sounds promising, Cheesewell. Bring it down. Let's examine it."

Cammy jumped to her feet. "It's up so high," she said, gazing up at the top shelf. "I'm not sure I can reach it."

"Bring that ladder over," Beef instructed, pointing to the tall, wooden library ladder leaning against a bookshelf on the opposite wall.

Cammy obediently hurried across the room and wheeled the ladder to the shelves next to Hardy's armchair. Then she climbed up quickly to retrieve the large book.

"Whoa. Careful," Hardy warned, craning his

neck to look up at her. "That ladder is very unsteady."

"Thanks for worrying about me," Cammy called down to him. He really *does* care about me, she thought.

"I just don't want you to fall on my head," Hardy said. "I have my hair brushed to perfect Academy specifications, and I don't want it mussed."

Cammy pulled the big book from the top shelf. Then felt herself slipping.

"Uh-oh!" she cried as she toppled off the top rung of the ladder.

The book hit the floor, and Cammy landed with a *plop* in Beef Hardy's lap.

"Whoa!" Hardy cried in surprise.

Stunned, Cammy put her arms around his neck in an attempt to get up.

She was still in this position as Commander Dorque bounced into the library, looking for a good mystery to read in bed.

"Cadet Hardy!" Dorque screamed, his bulbous face turning scarlet, his chins sagging as his mouth popped open in shock. "I don't believe what I'm seeing!"

"Uh . . . we're hard at work, sir," Hardy said, trying unsuccessfully to push Cammy up from his lap.

"I can *see* that!" the Commander cried. "I am

extremely disappointed in both of you!"

"I — I can explain, sir," Hardy stammered. "She isn't *really* sitting in my lap. She fell out of the sky! I mean — "

But the Commander had already spun around and furiously bounced back out the door.

They both stared at the doorway for a long moment. Then, Cammy, her arms still around Beef's neck, said apologetically, "I'm sorry. I guess we made a slight B-O-O B-O-O."

"Huh?" Hardy asked.

# 5

THE FOUR SPACE CADETS walked around the rifle practice field, thinking hard, but without success. It was a clear, warm night illuminated by a full moon and thousands of stars. But no bright ideas occurred to any of them.

"I still think we should do a project," Shaky insisted.

"What kind of a project?" Rip repeated for the hundredth time.

"Just a project!" Shaky replied defensively. "We could start it and see what develops. We don't have to know what it is in advance, do we?"

"I think we should build an android," Andy suggested. "A girl android. A real knockout. With long, blonde simulated hair and big blue glass eyes, and a rotary engine with — "

"Give us a break, Andy," Hunk interrupted.

"Just trying to be helpful," Andy said.

"Let's go in," Rip urged dispiritedly. "We're not getting any ideas out here. And I'm starving.

It's been a whole hour since dinner."

The four buddies trudged back inside and stopped outside the mess hall door. All of the lights were on in the vast dining room. There was no one in there.

"Let's just grab a little snack," Rip whispered, squeezing his massive belly through the door. "No one will know."

"Rip wants to get extra credit for *eating*," Hunk whispered.

"We shouldn't be in here. We're going to get in trouble," Shaky warned, glancing nervously behind them as they silently made their way across the mess hall to the kitchen.

Andy beeped and gave the time and temperature.

"Sshhh!" Shaky hissed.

"I can't help it," Andy explained. "I'm programmed to do that on the hour and half hour."

"And I'm programmed to eat on the hour and half hour," Rip proclaimed.

They stopped outside the kitchen and, huddled together, peered through the round window in the door. No one inside. Silently, they pushed open the swinging door and entered the brightly lit kitchen.

"If we're caught in here . . ." Shaky started.

But it was too late for warnings. Rip and Hunk had bounded into the pantry behind the kitchen and were already devouring a strawberry pie, scooping up big handfuls with their hands.

"Oh, I don't like this!" Shaky wailed, glancing nervously back at the door.

"Look what's for lunch tomorrow," Andy said. He was holding up the lid of a stainless-steel soup pot the size of a garbage can.

"What is it?" Rip called from the pantry, thick strawberry goo running down his chin onto the front of his uniform shirt.

"Pea soup," Andy announced, peering down into the giant pot.

"Yuck!" the other three cried in unison.

Pea soup was the least-favorite lunch of all the cadets at the Space Academy. As concocted by Carmella Flan, the cook, it was watery and bitter. It looked like something that had backed up from a sewer, and tasted almost as good.

"There are two things I hate about the food in the mess hall," Rip said, wiping his sticky mouth and chin with his shirtsleeve. "One — the food is disgusting. And, two — they give you such small portions!"

"But the pea soup is the worst, man," Hunk said unhappily.

Andy beeped loudly. "I have an idea!" he cried excitedly. "An extra-credit idea."

"Huh?" The other three gathered around him, Rip carrying the remains of the pie into the kitchen with him.

"I just searched my memory bank and found

47

a recipe for pea soup," Andy said. "What if I fixed the soup for tomorrow's lunch?"

"What are you talking about, man?" Hunk asked, his handsome face screwed up in confusion.

"I'll add some ingredients to the soup," Andy said excitedly. "I'll make it thicker. Make it taste sweet. I'll make it *good*."

"I get it!" Shaky cried. "Then when everyone likes it, when everyone sees how much improved it is, we'll step forward and admit that we're responsible for improving the soup."

"And we get extra credit!" Rip added, a pleased grin on his pie-stained face.

"Yo — even Commander Dorque hates the pea soup," Hunk said thoughtfully. "If we made it good, he'd be really grateful. I'll bet we *would* get extra credit! Andy — you're a genius, man!" He gave Andy a big bear hug, accidentally bending several important inner gears.

"Okay, let me get to work," Andy said, squeaking slightly, recovering slowly from the hug. "You guys go on upstairs. I'll fix the soup."

"Hey — don't you want us to stay and help?" Rip asked, eyeing another pie in the pantry.

"No," Andy insisted, motioning them away. "You know the old saying — 'Too many cooks spoil the horse.' "

Andy's old saying didn't make much sense to the other three, but they were used to it. Sometimes Andy would go entire days without making sense.

"Okay, we're going, man," Hunk said, heading toward the kitchen door. "But just make sure you do a good job. We want all the credit we deserve for this."

"No problem," Andy declared jauntily. And as his three friends departed, he reached under the sink for the ingredients he needed.

Later that night, several hours after Lights Out, Cadet Beef Hardy couldn't sleep. He sat straight up in bed and glanced around the darkened dorm room. This was unusual for Hardy. He always got the regulation eight-and-three-quarters hours of sleep, lying on his left side for exactly half that time period before rolling onto his right side for the remainder, his chin guard snapped in place to prevent snoring, as described in the Space Academy Regulation Book.

But tonight Hardy couldn't sleep, and he knew why.

He had embarrassed himself in front of the Academy Commander. Tonight he had disgraced himself, disgraced his uniform, and disgraced his school.

And even more importantly, he had wrecked the zipper on his pants, trying to pull out the shirt flap.

Commander Dorque is counting on me, and I

let him down, Hardy thought sadly, punching himself in the face several times to teach himself a lesson. Well, I won't let him down again.

He finished off with a couple of hard slaps, deciding to go easy on himself.

Tomorrow I will act, he told himself.

Tomorrow, Hardy knew, the visiting film crew was scheduled to be in the mess hall during lunch. The four Space Cadets were so noisy, so ill-mannered and disgusting, so piggish at every lunchtime, they were bound to draw the attention of the filmmakers.

But Beef Hardy was determined to keep the Space Cadets out of the mess hall. It wouldn't be hard. It wouldn't take any complicated plan.

A sneer formed on Hardy's cold, hard face. His P-O-O would be quite simple. His M-O-O would be easy as pie.

Just before lunch at 1200 hours, he'd send a note to Hunk and his friends, telling them they were needed urgently somewhere far from the mess hall. Let's see . . . where to send them?

To the spaceship launching hangar.

Yes. Of course. It was miles away. By the time those four clowns walked there, found there was no one waiting for them, and walked back, lunch would be over, and the film crew would be gone.

Mission accomplished.

At least for that one hour.

Then Hardy and Cheesewell would have to

get together again to come up with a long-range P-O-O. Or a W-T-K-T-S-C-F-G-I-T-F, or whatever the letters were.

Smiling to himself, feeling a little more reassured, Hardy fluffed his pillow to the regulation height of eight-point-seven centimeters, then drifted off into a peaceful, dreamless sleep.

"The pea soup tastes unusual today," Hunk heard Commander Dorque say. "Very tangy."

Hunk watched the headmaster slurp up the thick, green soup as he and his three friends hurried unhappily from the mess hall.

"There won't be any soup left by the time we get back!" Rip griped.

"What can we do, man?" Hunk replied, leading the way out of the mess hall and down the corridor. "This note says it's urgent that we report to the spaceship launching hangar."

"They seem to be enjoying my soup," Andy said, beaming happily, his eyes rolling wildly in his head.

"And we're missing it," Rip groaned. "Let me see that note. Who signed it?"

Hunk, walking quickly, removed the note from his pocket and studied it. "It's signed 'Corporal Ben Dover.' Ever hear of him?"

"Ben Dover?" Rip thought about the name. "Sounds familiar, but I just can't place it."

"Wait for me!" Shaky cried, hurrying to keep

up with Hunk's long strides. "I hope we aren't in any kind of trouble."

It took several minutes to walk to the hangar. Then it took several minutes to discover that the note must have been a mistake. Then it took several minutes to walk back to the mess hall.

By the time the Space Cadets returned, the vomiting was just beginning.

As they stepped into the room, they saw Cadet Beef Hardy lurch to his feet and begin to retch. Across the room at the officers' table, Commander Dorque was bent over double, spraying his green lunch all over the floor.

Within seconds, the vast room echoed with the most violent, disturbing groans, cries, and whimpers as the cadets heaved up their lunches, the thick pea-green substance pouring out their noses, gushing from their open mouths.

As the gagging and retching, gasping and moaning continued, the camera crew busily recorded the entire scene. "Good footage! Good footage!" Hunk heard one of the camera guys cry enthusiastically.

Hunk turned quickly to Andy. "Yo — think there's something wrong with your soup?" he asked, having to yell over the violent sounds that filled the room.

Andy shrugged. "I can't imagine," he told Hunk. "I only added one ingredient. A sweetener."

"What sweetener?" Rip asked.

"It's called Laundry Starch," Andy replied. "It helps to thicken the soup, and it makes it sweeter."

"Laundry starch?!" Hunk gaped at Andy, dumbfounded.

"Yes," Andy said innocently. "Don't you care for it? I always carry some with me — you know, for my sweet tooth." He produced a small box from his inside jacket pocket, took a pinch of powder, and tossed it into his mouth. "Mmmmm. It's good for your ball bearings, too," he said, sucking hard, then swallowing.

Across the room, Cadet Beef Hardy was being sick all over himself. Cadets were moaning and rolling on the floor. The cameras were whirring.

"Yo . . . Andy," Hunk said confidentially, leaning close to his friend's ear.

"Yes?" the android asked.

"I think maybe we'd better not tell anyone that we were responsible for changing the soup."

"No?" Andy looked surprised.

"But what about our extra credit?" Rip demanded.

# 6

COMMANDER DORQUE DIDN'T CARE about the blistering heat. The fresh air was making him feel better, reviving him, helping his stomach to settle. And walking through the field, observing the new leafy, green sprouts, renewed his spirit, gave him something to live for.

Sweet potato pudding.

Staring at the fragile, young leaves just lifting themselves up through the soil, he could taste the warm pudding already. So sweet. So lumpy. So chewy you could barely swallow it.

The Commander sighed, wiping his perspiring forehead with an already-soaked handkerchief. The week had not been going well. And it was all because of that pesky film crew and their stupid documentary.

Why did they always seem to be around with their cameras ready to go when embarrassing things happened?

And why were so many embarrassing things happening?

Scenes of the recent pea soup incident in the mess hall flashed through the Commander's troubled mind. They're not going to put that in the film — *are* they? he wondered.

A dark scowl crossed his face as he thought about it. The Space Cadets — they had to be responsible, he told himself. It had to be their doing.

After all, those four were the only ones who hadn't eaten the soup. They mysteriously had chosen to leave the dining hall when the soup was served. And as a result, they were the only ones who didn't get sick.

It wasn't an accident. It *couldn't* have been. Those four idiots knew what they were doing.

If only I had proof, the Commander thought, shaking his head miserably. If only I could catch them just once. . . .

Cadet Hardy had let him down, he thought darkly. The headmaster had given him an important assignment, and Hardy had chosen instead to loll about in the library with that redheaded cadet on his lap.

Commander Dorque had spoken harshly to Hardy right after lunch. But both of them were still feeling the ill effects of the pea soup, and Dorque wasn't sure he had gotten his message across.

His message had been: "Don't let me down again."

Hardy had assured the headmaster that he wouldn't. And then he had saluted so hard that he required six stitches.

Dignity, Dorque thought, bending to sniff a sweet potato leaf. All we need around this place is a little dignity.

He patted his bald head dry with the handkerchief. The sun was getting too strong. It was time to go back inside.

The low pile of fertilizer lay festering in the sun just ahead of him. Remembering what had happened last time, Commander Dorque gazed up at the low tree limb above his head, eager to avoid it.

Since he was looking up, he didn't see the small, round hole at his feet. Stepping forward quickly, his foot got caught in the hole, and he fell face forward into the fertilizer.

After Lights Out that night, Cadet Beef Hardy silently crept out of his dorm room and made his way through the dimly lit, empty corridors to the library, his arranged meeting place with Cadet Cheesewell.

His eyes darting quickly through the room, making sure that it was vacant, Hardy began to pace angrily along the wall of books.

Hardy had been angry ever since that afternoon when he'd been chewed out by Commander Dorque. He realized he was angry at himself, mostly, for embarrassing himself in front of the Commander, for letting the Commander down.

Right after his talk with the Commander, Hardy had punched out a couple of plebes, smashed some ribs, broken a few noses. But it didn't do much to soothe his feelings.

Now, waiting for Cammy to arrive, he gave himself a hard punch in the stomach as a reminder to himself of just how angry he was.

He was still gasping, doubled over from the effects of the punch, when Cammy Cheesewell entered the library. She looked radiant, her red hair pinned on top of her head in a soft bun, her green eyes glowing in the dim library light.

She gave him a warm smile and hurried over to where he was grasping a chair arm, trying to regain his breath. He saw that she was carrying a bundle of some sort in one arm.

"What's that?" he asked her, sliding into the armchair.

She held it up. "It's just a skirt. I'm hemming it. I thought I'd work on it while we chatted." Once again, she sat down in the big armchair opposite his. She arranged her skirt on her lap and began working on it with a needle and thread.

"We're not here to chat," Beef said stiffly. "This is an emergency, Cadet Cheesewell."

"Yes, sir," she said, giving him a salute with the hand holding the needle.

"We have to go into emergency mode," Hardy said seriously.

"Ouch," she replied, having poked her thumb with the needle.

"I've been studying military tactics all afternoon and all evening," Hardy told her, watching the needle move expertly in and out as she stitched. "I've been studying containment techniques and methods of enemy rejection and dispersement. And after reading what the great military minds have written, I think I have a plan that will help us against the Space Cadets."

"What's that?" she asked, looking up from her work.

"We steal their pants," Beef Hardy said.

"Huh?" Cammy Cheesewell's mouth dropped open.

"It's a brilliant plan if I don't say so myself," Hardy said, leaning forward excitedly in the big armchair. "Tomorrow is the last day the camera crew is going to be filming. And tomorrow is the championship all-Academy intramural volleyball tournament."

"Yes, I know," Cammy said, returning to her hemming. "I've been practicing my serve all afternoon."

"Well, the camera crew will be filming the tournament," Hardy continued, ignoring her remark. "And we have to make sure the Space Cadets aren't there."

"They're always so disgusting at volleyball tournaments," Cammy said, making a face. "Always tossing the skinny one — Shaky — over the net and then batting him back and forth. They think that's such a riot!"

"We can't let them compete tomorrow," Hardy said, slapping the broad arm of the chair with determination. "So we'll steal their pants."

Cammy wrinkled her features in confusion. "You mean sneak into their room?"

"Yes," Hardy repeated impatiently, "and steal their pants. I'll wait till they're down having breakfast in the morning. Then I'll jimmy open the door, sneak in, raid their dressers, and steal their pants."

Cammy stared back at him, thinking hard. "But what about the pants they wear down to breakfast?" she asked.

Hardy's mouth dropped open. He slapped his forehead, realizing that she was right. "Good point," he told her admiringly. "Have you been reading the military books, too? I nearly made a major blunder."

"Glad I could be helpful," Cammy said, blushing prettily. "Why don't you sneak in before breakfast, while they're in the shower?"

"Brilliant!" Beef cried, jumping to his feet. "That's just what I'll do."

"Beef, since I helped you, would you do me a really big favor?" Cammy asked, bunching the skirt in her lap.

"Sure. If it doesn't break any rules or regulations," Hardy replied carefully. "Doing favors for another cadet is an important part of the cadets' conduct code, which I subscribe to in full."

"Well . . . it's a really big favor," Cammy said reluctantly, gazing hard into his steel-gray eyes.

"Go ahead and ask," Hardy said generously. "Thinking about those four losers trapped in their dorm room for the day with no pants to wear has put me in an exceptionally good mood."

"Well" — Cadet Cheesewell took a deep breath — "would you put on this skirt?"

"What?" Hardy shrieked.

"I can't get the hem straight. I need someone to try it on so I can repin it. You're about my height, and . . ." She held the skirt up to him.

"Whoa," Hardy cried, backing away. "I'm sorry, but I can't put on a skirt. Why don't you put it on yourself?"

"I can't wear it and pin it." Cammy sighed. "Come on, Beef. It'll take two minutes."

"But what if someone sees me?"

They both looked to the door. Outside, the shadowy hallway was still and silent.

"No one is awake," Cammy told him, whispering for some reason. "We're the only ones. No one will see. Please! Go behind that bookcase and put on the skirt. It'll be a really big help." Again, she held it up to him.

Beef Hardy shook his head. "No way."

"But what about the cadets' code of conduct? You said you subscribe to it fully."

Beef Hardy gulped, realizing she was leaving him no choice. He did subscribe to the cadets' code of conduct. When asked a favor by another cadet, he had to comply.

Glumly, he grabbed the skirt from her hands and trudged behind the bookcase to pull off his uniform trousers and put on the skirt.

I'll bet he looks adorable in it, Cammy thought giddily to herself. "You're being such a good sport, Beef," she called to him. "I'll pay you back for this favor. I'll meet you tomorrow morning and help you carry away all of their pants."

She could hear Beef muttering a reply from behind the bookcase, but she couldn't make out the words.

A few seconds later, he stepped out wearing the skirt. He walked awkwardly up to her armchair, his face red as a beet. "Okay. Just make this fast," he said through clenched teeth, holding his arms out stiffly at his sides.

Cammy admired Beef in the skirt, not a bit disappointed in how he looked. Even his surprisingly hairy legs did little to spoil her admiration. Sighing longingly, she lowered herself to her knees on the carpet and began to pin the hem.

Suddenly, about halfway round, she stopped. "I just thought of something," she said, staring up at him.

"What?" he asked impatiently, shifting his weight.

"The Space Cadets don't need pants to play in the volleyball tournament. They play in shorts."

"I have that covered," Hardy said confidently. "I plan to steal all of their shorts, too. And all of their undershorts."

"Oh, Beef, you're just so . . . amazing," Cammy gushed.

"And I plan to steal their towels, too," Beef continued. "And their drapes. And anything else they might try to wrap around them."

"You're absolutely brilliant," Cammy said, concentrating on pinning the hem. "One day *you* will be in those military books."

"Probably," Hardy replied.

"Where'd you get such hairy legs?" she asked. The words just slipped out. She hadn't intended to say that.

"Hairy legs run in my family," Hardy said. Having never made a joke in his life, he didn't realize that he had just made one. "I keep my leg hair at regulation length — two-point-six centimeters," he added proudly.

"Uh-oh," Cammy said, climbing to her feet with a groan. "Out of pins."

"What?"

"I'm out of pins. I'll be right back."

Hardy started to protest, but she was already running out the door. He moved awkwardly to the long reading table in the center of the room and glanced at the books that had been left out.

To his surprise, he liked the way the skirt felt as he walked. It gave him so much more freedom than his tight uniform slacks.

Some mighty warriors wore skirts, he thought, twirling around to see how it felt. Especially in Scotland. Those Scottish guys always wore skirts in battle, plaid skirts at that.

What was keeping Cadet Cheesewell?

Hardy glanced at the door, then twirled again.

Whee! It felt good.

The skirt billowed up around his legs.

Hardy was still twirling and the skirt was still billowing when Commander Dorque walked into the library, looking for something to read to put him to sleep.

He took a step, then stopped in the doorway, and his mouth dropped nearly to the floor. "Hardy!" he bellowed.

Cadet Hardy stopped twirling. Seeing the Commander standing there, hands on hips, his eyes bulging, glaring at him in shock and disbelief, he suddenly felt very dizzy.

"Hardy!" Commander Dorque repeated. He opened his mouth as if he wanted to say more, but no words came out. His eyes seemed to be frozen at Hardy's knees.

"Uh . . . I can explain, sir," Hardy stammered. Commander Dorque remained frozen in astonishment.

"Hairy legs run in my family," Hardy said, by way of explanation.

# 7

Three hours earlier, the four Space Cadets had been in their dorm room, restlessly pondering the day's events, trying to figure out what to do next.

"Put me down! Put me down!" Shaky cried, flailing out his bony arms and kicking with his bony legs.

"No way," Rip told him. "Tomorrow's the big volleyball tournament, isn't it?"

"Yeah. So?" Shaky wailed.

"So I've got to practice my serve." Holding Shaky in the palm of his left hand, Rip brought his hammy right fist up hard underneath his quivering friend and sent him sailing across the room into the wall.

"Too low," Rip grumbled. "That would be a net ball. Let me try again."

"Oh, no!" Shaky cried. He struggled to his feet, looking a lot like a panicked grasshopper, and scrambled out of Rip's grasp.

"Yo — let him go," Hunk called from the couch near the window. "Practice your serve later, man. We've got some heavy thinking to do."

"Ha-ha-ho-ho. That's the *only* kind of thinking Rip can do!" Andy cracked.

Rip glared at him. "Knock off the fat jokes, or I'll sit on your gearbox."

"Rip is so heavy," Andy joked, "when he walks, his shoes cry, 'Avalanche! Avalanche!' "

Andy laughed uproariously, slapping his synthetic-plastic knees, but nobody else laughed. Andy's jokes were terrible. But he thought he was hilarious.

"If you don't shut up, I'm going to turn your head around so you walk into yourself!" Rip threatened Andy.

"Yo — come *on,* guys," Hunk pleaded impatiently. "We've got to concentrate. We've got to think about how we're going to get that extra credit we need."

"Rip doesn't need extra credit. He already has extra chins!" Andy cracked, and then laughed for nearly a minute. "Do you know why Rip is fat?" Andy asked. "Because he weighs a lot!" He laughed so hard, he squeaked.

Rip turned eagerly to Hunk. "Hey, Hunk, give me permission to take him down to the warehouse and sell him for parts."

"Rip is so fat, he doesn't have a waist. He has

66

a *circumference*!" Andy cried, cracking himself up again.

Rip moved forward, about to grab Andy by the neck. Hunk held up a hand, signaling for him to stop. "Hey, Rip, I almost forgot," Hunk said, pulling a white envelope out from his back pants pocket. "This came for you while you were down in the mess hall this afternoon, scrounging around on the floor for crumbs the cleanup squad missed."

Rip pulled the envelope from Hunk's hand. His face lit up. "Hey — it's a letter from my kid brother Flathead!"

"Great!" Shaky cried, crawling back into the room. Everyone huddled around Rip. They all enjoyed listening to letters from Rip's brother back home.

Rip eagerly unfolded the handwritten letter and began to read.

" 'Dear Amerylus Lucretius,' the letter begins," said Rip, squinting to make out the words.

"Hey — why does your brother call you Amerylus Lucretius?" Hunk asked.

"I don't think he knows how to spell Rip," was Rip's reply. He continued reading:

*Things are okay back home.*
*Mom was a little depressed when the bottom fell out of the used-tissue market. She was hoping to clean up*

with used tissues, but instead she was just about wiped out.

She's been busy doing a lot of canning and putting up preserves, getting ready for winter. We had a little setback when the dog got in Mom's way. You know what a pest Princess could be! We're not quite sure which jars Princess is in. But I'm sure we'll find out once we start to eat this winter.

Dad is doing much better since he finally found a hobby. Mom's been after him for years to find a new hobby, ever since he got too old for his old hobby of chasing after cars. (It used to be a hoot in the old days to see Dad and Princess chasing after the same car — wasn't it, bro? Especially the looks on the drivers' faces.)

Anyway, Dad's got a more relaxing hobby now. He's collecting bruises. He's got quite a collection already — two beauties on his arm, and a real prizewinner on his forehead. We're all so proud of him.

We're real proud of you, too, bro. Thanks for stealing that real spacegun from the Academy and sending it to me. You knew it was just what I wanted. It's deadly! And what a practical birthday present! I already used it to put a little scare on my teacher. Thanks to you, bro, I think my grades are gonna go straight up!

Don't worry about Louie, your hamster. I've been feeding him five times a day just like you said. Only problem is, I haven't seen Louie for a while. I left the cage right near where Mom was doing her canning and preserves and haven't seen him since. But no sweat — I'm sure he'll turn up.

*It's Dad's birthday next week. It's a big secret, so don't tell him, okay? I think I'm going to give him a new bruise.*

*Take care of yourself, bro. I'll write again real soon.*

Love,
Flathead

A teary smile on his face, Rip glanced over the letter one more time, then folded it and tucked it into his shirt pocket.

"Hey — how come your brother is named Flathead?" Hunk asked.

Rip shrugged. "No reason *not* to call him that," he replied.

Hunk thought about the answer for a while, then shook his head hard as if clearing his brain. "Come on, guys. Let's think about what we're going to do for extra credit."

"How about a project?" Andy chimed in immediately.

"Yeah," Rip agreed, to everyone's surprise. "I have a great idea for a project. It's 'How to Dismantle an Android.' "

"Give Andy a break!" Shaky cried, stepping protectively in front of Andy.

Andy beeped and gave the time and temperature.

"It's getting late," Hunk said. "Let's take another walk. Maybe it'll give us another idea." He stood up quickly and headed toward the door.

"We didn't get such a good idea the *last* time we took a walk," Shaky said, his expression tense.

"Yeah. Let's stay in and practice our volleyball serve," Rip said, eyeing Shaky.

"On second thought, let's take a walk," Shaky said, hurrying to catch up with Hunk.

They wandered through the dormitory halls for a while, which were empty and silent. Most cadets were busily studying in their rooms.

No extra-credit ideas came to mind. They decided to take the elevator down to the first floor. As they waited at the elevator bank, Debby Dorque came hurrying by, carrying a stack of candy bars her dad had requested, her blonde hair trailing behind her like a shimmering wave of wheat, her blue eyes sparkling even brighter than usual as she spotted Hunk.

She smiled at him, and then her expression turned reproachful. "Did you guys follow my advice? Have you started an extra-credit project?" she asked, staring into Hunk's eyes.

He smiled at her, his best 352-tooth smile.

I'd give him extra credit for that smile *any time*, Debby thought.

He turned his left profile toward her. He knew it was his best side.

"Well?" she asked, glowing all over. The candy bars were melting from the heat of her hands.

"Could you repeat the question?" he asked, in his deepest, most manly voice.

"I forget it," she said sighing dreamily. She forced herself to snap out of her trance. "I asked you about extra credit."

"Oh, yes." Hunk tried to snap his fingers, but missed. He never could get the hang of it. Do you snap your pointer finger or your middle finger against your thumb? How do you get it to make a noise?

"We're looking for a project right now," Rip said. "Can I help you carry those candy bars?" He reached out to take them from her, but she pulled away.

"Good luck, guys," Debby Dorque said, taking one last, long look at Hunk's beautiful, open-mouthed face, and then hurried off to the Commander's office.

"We've got to find a project. We've just *got* to," Hunk said, watching her walk away. "I don't want to flunk out."

The elevator doors opened, and they rode quickly down to the lobby. Stepping out, their shoes clattered noisily on the marble floors, echoing across the wide lobby.

It was completely deserted down there. The front doors were shut and locked. The building was closed to all visitors. The officers and cadets were all upstairs on the dormitory floors.

It was the perfect place to walk. And think.

Extra credit. Extra credit. Extra credit.

"Should we do a project?" Andy suggested brightly, as if thinking of it for the first time.

The other three ignored him.

They crossed the wide hall, and then stopped at the far wall in front of the enormous, ancient, priceless mural that had been lent to the Academy by the Schnauzers.

The four Space Cadets, naturally, hadn't been invited to the unveiling of the mural. And, so, this was the first time they were seeing it.

"Look at that!" Shaky cried, pointing.

"Man, I don't believe it!" Rip exclaimed, gaping.

"Wow! Wow spelled backward!" Andy declared.

"Yo! Somebody spray-painted graffiti all over the lobby wall," Hunk said, staring at it hard, trying to make out some of the sayings and slogans.

"How awful!" Shaky added.

"Some clown sure did a job on the wall, all right," Rip agreed. "Phew! What a mess!"

"It's just scrawls," Shaky agreed, moving closer, squinting through his glasses, unable to read a word of it.

"Just ugly scrawls," Andy said. "It doesn't make any sense."

"It's not even funny!" Rip complained.

"I rather like the swirling brushstroke technique in that corner," Andy said, pointing. "It's an interesting balance of light and perspective, don't you agree?"

"Some creep just went wild with a spray can," Hunk said, shaking his head. "Who could have done it?"

"It *had* to be one of us," Rip said. "No one else would do a thing like this."

They all stared at each other accusingly. Then all of them began denying it at once.

"When Commander Dorque lays his eyes on this mess, he'll explode!" Hunk exclaimed.

"He'll probably put the whole school on report," Shaky said unhappily.

"He might make us go without dessert," Rip added.

"Yo! I've got it!" Hunk shouted, startling his three companions.

"Huh?" All three cried as one.

"This is it!" Hunk cried. "Our extra-credit project. We'll clean this up right now. Then tomorrow morning, we'll go tell Commander Dorque. He'll be so happy that we cleaned up this eyesore, he'll give us extra credit on the spot!"

"Yes! Yes!" cried Andy, enthusiastically slapping himself a high-five.

"It might be hard to clean up," Shaky said, staring up at the black scrawls and crude drawings that nearly covered the entire lobby wall.

Rip stepped right up to it and rubbed a finger over some of the markings. Then he rubbed his big hand over it, smearing it just a little. "Yeah," he agreed. "It'll take months to wash this gunk off. It's sprayed on real good."

"Then we'll paint over it!" Hunk suggested.

"Yes! Yes!" Andy agreed, slapping himself a low-five.

"What color should we paint it?" Rip asked.

"How about silver and gold, the color of an android's heart?" Andy asked.

Everyone ignored him, as usual.

"The other walls are all brown," Shaky said, turning to examine them. "Sort of a brown-brown."

"I know where the paint is kept," Rip said. "I was looking for a late-night snack one night and I stumbled into the paint storage closet. We can find the right shade there. There are brushes and stuff in the closet, too."

"All right!" Hunk declared enthusiastically. "Let's go, guys!"

A few minutes later, the four Space Cadets carried down several gallons of paint. Then, fat paintbrushes in hand, they began covering the ancient mural with a thick coat of brown. Sort of a brown-brown.

It didn't take long. Even with time out for a short but satisfying paint fight.

Fifteen minutes later, their work completed, the four paint-drenched friends put down their brushes and stepped back to admire their handiwork.

"Perfect," Hunk declared.

"It looks like all the other walls," Rip said happily. "You can't tell there was any graffiti there."

"Commander Dorque will *have* to give us extra credit for this job!" Shaky exclaimed happily.

"Yes, we're bound to get it," Andy agreed.

# 8

"ARE YOU SURE they're in the shower?" Cammy whispered.

"Yes, I'm sure," Beef whispered back. "Listen."

It was the next morning, and Cammy and Beef were huddled in front of the Space Cadets' doorway, preparing to sneak inside.

Down the hall, they could hear the hiss of water in the shower room and the unmistakable sound of slapping towels.

Cammy nodded her head, reassured. It had to be the four Space Cadets in the shower room. They were the only ones who could not take a shower without slapping each other with wet towels.

Hardy turned the knob, and the two of them pushed their way into the room. Silently, they moved quickly across the floor, cluttered with books and papers, candy wrappers, and assorted garbage, through the front room to the bedroom in the back.

There were small, white feathers everywhere, on the beds, on the dressertops, on the area rug in the center of the bedroom — evidence that a heavy-duty pillow fight had taken place the night before.

"It looks like it snowed in here!" Cammy exclaimed.

"Shh. Let's just grab all of their pants and get out," Beef urged, pulling open a dresser drawer. "Phew!" He cringed and drew back, holding his nose. "It smells like someone died in there."

They both took deep breaths and held them, then began pulling pants and shorts from the drawers as quickly as they could, piling them over their shoulders. "Don't they have any *clean* clothes?" Cammy asked, trying not to inhale.

"Hurry," Beef urged. He pulled open another drawer, reached inside, screamed, and jerked his hand out.

"Beef? What's wrong?" Cammy asked.

"Sorry." He lifted out a dead mouse, dangling it by the tail. By the looks of it, it had been dead for weeks. "I guess they left that in there to freshen up the smell of their clothes," he said, dropping it back into the drawer.

Cammy gagged. "I'm going to be sick."

"Just keep piling up the pants. We're almost finished," Hardy said, emptying the drawer and moving on to the next. "I've got to prove to Commander Dorque that he can rely on me. I kind of got the feeling when he saw me wearing your skirt last night that he was beginning to lose confidence in me."

They emptied the dresser drawers, piling more pants and shorts and undershorts on their shoulders. Then they searched the rest of the room, sifting through the thick layer of feathers, making sure they got everything.

"Okay. Mission accomplished," Hardy said, groaning under the weight of the huge mountain of clothing he carried. "Let's go before they come back."

He and Cadet Cheesewell were nearly to the front door when it opened and Andy entered, still wet from the shower, a large white bath towel wrapped around his waist.

"Hi," Andy said, smiling, raising one hand in greeting, the other hand holding the towel together. He couldn't see who the intruders were. Their faces were hidden behind the high piles of pants.

"Good morning," Hardy muttered, disguising his voice, careful to keep his face hidden from view. He glanced over at Cammy, who was also cowering behind the stolen clothes, her features locked in fear.

"Can I help you?" Andy asked, confused.

"Uh . . . we're just collecting some things for the cadet rummage sale," Hardy said, thinking quickly.

"Oh, really?" Andy replied. "Well, here. Take this, too." He removed the towel and tossed it on top of Cammy's clothing collection.

Commander Donald Dorque had a wide smile on his round airbag of a face. The thing he liked best about visitors was when they left. And the delegation of Schnauzers was about to leave the Academy and return to their home planet.

Their visit had been brief but pleasant. And now their bags were packed, and the Commander was eagerly looking forward to his favorite part of any visit — saying good-bye.

If only that idiotic film crew would go with them, he thought, walking briskly through the lobby hallway, accompanying the leader of the Schnauzer party. What a nuisance those film-makers had been. At least, thought the head-master, today is their last day here. After the cadet volleyball tournament, they'd be packing up their equipment and heading back to headquarters.

So far, so good, the Commander thought uneasily. He had been worried about being em-barrassed in the film. But so far, nothing too terrible had occurred.

If Hardy succeeds at keeping the Space Cadets out of the volleyball tournament, I can breathe easy, he thought.

"Commander Dorque? Commander Dorque?"

The headmaster suddenly realized that the Schnauzer leader was trying to get his attention. "It's pronounced Dor*kay*," he corrected his guest.

I don't care if you are a fat, grinning rhinoceros, Dorque thought, a phony grin plastered on his face, at least you can learn to pronounce my name correctly.

"Just one last look at our precious mural," the Schnauzer requested, pleading with his watery eyes.

"Of course," Commander Dorque said grandly, gesturing across the hall. One last look, and then *scram*.

He led the way, followed by eight large Schnauzers clumping noisily across the lobby floor.

"We will miss the mural so much in my country," the leader said sadly. "It means so much to me and to all of my Schnauzers. But at least we will have the knowledge that this priceless work is in good hands."

"Yeah, right," Commander Dorque agreed, not really listening, his mind on other matters, namely his breakfast.

They stopped in front of the mural.

There was a long silence. The air seemed to freeze.

The only sounds were loud gasps of surprise.

"You took the mural down?" the Schnauzer leader asked the Commander, his expression revealing his astonishment.

"No, of course not," Commander Dorque replied, staring at the brown wall, trying to figure out exactly what was happening.

They all took a step closer. They all inspected the wall carefully.

On an impulse, Commander Dorque reached a finger out and touched the wall. The paint was sticky. Fresh.

His heart seemed to stop. He couldn't breathe. Staring straight ahead, his eyes glazing over in disbelief, he suddenly realized what they were all gaping at.

It was the ancient, priceless mural. Painted brown.

"Ha-ha." Nervous laughter escaped his choked throat. "Someone's made a little boo-boo here," he said, smiling in the hopes of covering up his real feelings. And then, for some reason, more laughter escaped. "Ha-ha-ha!" He couldn't control it.

The Schnauzers, needless to say, were not laughing. "A boo-boo?" their leader asked, his eyes turning red. The hard, bony plates down his back rose and stiffened.

"Someone seems to have painted over it," Commander Dorque said, his chins starting to quiver. Seeing the furious, fierce expressions on his guests' faces, he took a step back. "Ha-ha-ha!" Why couldn't he stifle that hideous laughter?

"The color brown is an *insult* in my country!"

the Schnauzer leader bellowed, his powerful voice ringing through the vast lobby. "The color brown is the *worst* insult, even worse than insulting someone's mother!"

"Ha-ha-ha," Commander Dorque laughed weakly, taking another step back, bullets of sweat pouring down his forehead.

"Of course," screamed the enraged Schnauzer, "this means *war*!"

"Ha-ha-ha!" the headmaster replied.

# 9

COMMANDER DORQUE WAS LEANING over his desk, holding his head in his hands and moaning softly, when Cadet Hardy entered the office later that afternoon. Hardy saluted and waited for the headmaster to respond.

He waited nearly a minute and then, realizing that the Commander was not going to respond, Hardy cleared his throat and broke the silence. "I came to report on my mission, sir," Hardy said in a chipper tone. "I believe it went well."

"Hunnnnnnh," was all the Commander could manage as a reply.

"What was that, sir?" Hardy asked, stepping closer in an attempt to hear the headmaster more clearly.

"Hunnnnnnnh," Dorque repeated, his black, beady eyes rolling around in their red-rimmed sockets.

"Hunnnnnh?"

"Hunnnnnh," came the reply.

"Should I take that to mean you're pleased with my efforts?" Hardy asked hopefully.

"Hunnnnnh," Commander Dorque replied. Then he pitched forward onto the desktop and appeared to be unconscious for several minutes.

Hardy waited patiently. He had no choice. The Commander hadn't dismissed him. According to Rule 344, Hardy couldn't leave the office without a salute of dismissal.

I wonder if he's dead, Hardy thought, gaping at the headmaster, who was sprawled facedown on top of his papers.

If he's dead, do I still have to wait for a salute of dismissal?

After a while, much to Hardy's relief, Commander Dorque seemed to revive. He pulled himself to his feet, straightened his necktie, and, sighing weakly, plopped into his desk chair.

He gazed at Hardy for the longest time, as if trying to get him in focus. "Hardy," he said finally, rubbing his temples, "did you manage to keep the Space Cadets out of the volleyball tournament?"

"I believe so, sir," Hardy replied, stiffening to attention. "I had a foolproof strategy, sir. I believe it must have succeeded."

"You weren't at the volleyball tournament?" Dorque asked suspiciously.

"No, sir," Hardy told him. "I . . . uh . . . had to take a shower all afternoon . . . to . . . uh . . .

84

get rid of the smell from some clothes I borrowed."

"Hunnnnnh," Dorque replied, seeming to slip
back toward unconsciousness again.

"Sir, is something troubling you?" Hardy asked
uncertainly.

"Hunnnnh," Dorque said, closing his eyes,
swaying from side to side in the big desk chair.
"The film."

Hardy struggled to understand what the Commander was saying. "Film?"

Dorque pointed weakly to a movie projector
set up on the other side of the office, pointing at
a small movie screen.

"You're looking at a film? A movie?" Hardy
guessed.

"Hunnnnnh," Dorque said.

"Huh?"

"Hunnnnnh."

"Huh?"

"The filmmakers," Dorque explained. "They
brought a rough cut of their film for me to see.
Before they take it back to headquarters."

"That was nice of them," Hardy commented.

"I hope so," Dorque replied. "This hasn't been
the best of days." He stood up and walked across
the room, beckoning for Cadet Hardy to join
him. "Sit down. We'll watch the film together,"
Dorque said. "We'll see how successful you were
in keeping the Space Cadets out of it."

Hardy drew up a straight-backed chair and sat down stiffly next to the headmaster. "I'm sure you'll be pleased with the film, sir," he said confidently.

Commander Dorque made a face, then shouted into the outer office. "Miss Moon — come in here and run the projector for us!"

After a brief hesitation, Miss Moon's voice floated in from the other side of the door. "I don't know how, sir!"

"Never mind!" Dorque shouted back. "I'll do it myself."

"If you wish!" Miss Moon replied.

Groaning, the Commander got up, crossed the room to switch off the lights, then crossed back and clicked on the movie projector. Light flickered over the silver movie screen. Colonel Dorque, groaning once again, plopped back in his seat.

"What's the movie called, sir?" Cadet Hardy asked, staring at the shimmering light on the screen.

"I'm not sure. Something like 'A Day at the Space Academy,'" Dorque told him. "I told you, Hardy — it's going to be shown as a public relations film all over the galaxy. That's why I'm so eager for it to show us in a good light."

Both of them settled back as the screen darkened. The opening shot showed the tall glass-

and-steel Space Academy Building, sparkling in the sunlight. "Very impressive," Commander Dorque muttered, staring hard at the screen.

The next scene appeared to be outdoors somewhere. The tower could be seen in the far background. And there was Commander Dorque walking toward the camera. Suddenly he seemed to be caught by a low tree limb. He toppled over into a pile of fertilizer.

"Oh, no!" Dorque wailed, jumping to his feet, pointing to the screen.

There he was, floundering around in the dark fertilizer, struggling to his feet, covered from head to foot.

"Why'd they show that?" Hardy asked.

Commander Dorque, his eyes bulging like overripe plums, didn't seem to hear him.

The next scene was in the mess hall. In a rolling close-up, the four Space Cadets were drooling over their chins, allowing the thick slobber to drip down toward the floor.

"That's not my fault!" Hardy cried. "That was before I was on the case, sir."

Once again, Commander Dorque, gaping openmouthed at the screen, failed to reply.

The film crew cut from the drooling contest to another scene in the mess hall. Cadets were standing up, bending over, lurching about, vomiting up pea soup.

Hardy and the headmaster stared at this scene in disbelief. "Look — I believe that's you, sir," Hardy pointed out.

Sure enough, it was the Commander retching his guts out at the officers' table.

"You'd look very handsome if you weren't heaving up your lunch," Hardy complimented him. "You have a good face for the camera, sir."

Dorque didn't reply.

The dining hall scene faded. The gym came into view. There was a brief shot of the volleyball net strung in the center of the floor.

"Oh, look. The volleyball tournament," Hardy said enthusiastically. "Now we'll see how well my little scheme to keep the Space Cadets away succeeded, sir."

On the screen, the two teams of cadets began to play. A cadet served a high, arching serve that nearly hit the gym ceiling.

And then the four Space Cadets came into view.

"Huh? What are *they* doing there?" Hardy gasped, nearly toppling from his chair. "I thought — "

Hunk and his three friends, Hardy could see, were wearing regulation Academy athletic T-shirts. And they were wearing regulation Academy gym sneakers.

And in between the T-shirts and the sneakers,

they were wearing only baggy, red and white polka dot boxer shorts.

How on earth did I miss *those* beauties? Hardy thought.

"H-H-H-Hardy!" Commander Dorque bellowed, pointing furiously as the four Space Cadets enjoyed their game as if nothing was out of the ordinary. As if the cameras weren't rolling. As if the entire galaxy wouldn't be watching. "H-H-H-Hardy — they're *out of uniform!*"

"I see that, sir," Hardy replied weakly.

"But — where are their pants?"

"I stole them, sir," Hardy confessed. "To keep them out of the tournament."

"But they're *in* the tournament!" Dorque wailed, tearing at where his hair used to be. "Why are they in the tournament?"

"I guess they're completely shameless, sir," Hardy said, shrugging. "Who would have guessed?"

Commander Dorque leapt up and shot his fist at the movie screen. It made a dent but didn't break through. He turned off the projector, glaring at Hardy.

"But — but I will be court-martialed for this!" Dorque shrieked. "No. Court-martialing will be too good for me! When my superior officers see this film, I'll be fired. I'll be shot. I'll be hung. I'll be shot and then hung! I'll be a laughingstock over the entire galaxy!"

"Probably, sir," Hardy reluctantly replied.

"M-m-my career will be over!" stammered the headmaster. "I will be in disgrace. Utter disgrace. What can we do, Hardy? What can we do?"

"Hunnnnnh," Cadet Hardy told him in all honesty.

# 10

COMMANDER DORQUE, WEARY AND DEFEATED, his face collapsed nearly to his chest, stared bleakly at his desktop. Cadet Hardy stood frozen across the room, uncertain of what to do next.

Should he leave the Commander to his sadness and disgrace? Should he try to help? Or should he continue to stand there, frozen helplessly, wanting to scratch the back of his neck but not sure if this was the proper time and place?

"I'm ruined. Ruined . . ." Commander Dorque whimpered. He began to howl softly like a wounded puppy.

A knock on the office door startled them both. They were even more startled when Hunk poked his handsome, wavy-haired head jauntily into the room. "Sir, is this a good time?" Hunk asked.

The headmaster looked up at him weakly. "A good time?" He began whimpering a bit louder.

"Are you wearing trousers?" Cadet Hardy demanded of Hunk, sneering at him suspiciously.

Hunk stepped into the room. He was wearing standard uniform trousers. "I'll only take a minute, Commander Dorque," he said brightly. "I wanted to request extra credit for the work my friends and I did last night."

"Work?" Commander Dorque's face appeared to lift off his chest. He stared at Hunk with interest. "What kind of work?"

"Well, we were walking in the lobby last night, sir, when we saw something really gross," Hunk began, beaming with pride, eagerly anticipating his reward for a job well done.

"Your own reflection?" Hardy cracked.

"We found some graffiti, sir," Hunk continued, ignoring Beef. "Someone had spray-painted one whole wall down there. But we knew just what to do. We take pride in our Academy," Hunk said, pouring it on a bit thick in hopes of winning the extra credit. "We like to keep it looking right."

"Don't tell me," Commander Dorque said, sighing and shaking his head.

"So we got some brown paint and painted over the graffiti so the wall looked like new," Hunk continued.

"I *asked* you not to tell me!" Dorque cried, banging his head repeatedly against the desktop.

"We thought maybe you'd like to give us extra credit, sir," Hunk said, a little surprised at the Commander's head-banging reaction. "You know, for using our own initiative."

Commander Dorque banged his head against the desk for a few minutes more. Then he stood up, pulling himself up to his full height of four-foot-two, and his face turned crimson with fury as he prepared to tell Hunk that the firing squad would be the only kind of extra credit he and his friends would be receiving.

But before the Commander could speak, the phone on his desk rang, startling him so badly, he leapt onto his desk. "Out!" he shouted to both Hunk and Hardy. "Out of here! Both of you!"

Hardy slumped out, disappointed that Hunk didn't get his tongue-lashing. Hunk slumped out, disappointed that he didn't get his extra credit. The door closed behind them.

Trying to compose himself, Commander Dorque picked up the phone. His superior officer, General Innis Outt, was on the other end of the line.

It wasn't a social call. General Outt had serious news to report. Grim news. Dire news.

Commander Dorque listened quietly to the General's somber, urgent words. Then, his voice trembling, he told the General, "I will carry out your orders immediately, sir."

He hung up the receiver, thinking about the General's frightening news. Then he climbed up onto his desktop and did a joyful tap dance, waving his arms happily high above his head.

His dance completed, he jumped down from the desk and gleefully called Cadet Hardy back into the office. Hardy entered, and his face filled with surprise seeing the headmaster looking so rejuvenated.

"Hardy, wonderful news!" Dorque cried, clapping him enthusiastically on the back, so enthusiastically that Hardy went sailing into the wall.

"Uh, what's the wonderful news?" Hardy asked when he had peeled himself from the wallpaper.

"General Outt has just informed me that we must all evacuate the Space Academy at once! The Schnauzers were serious about their declaration of war! They're on their way in war crafts right now! They're coming to destroy the Space Academy! Isn't that wonderful, my boy?"

Dorque clapped Hardy on the back again, this time sending him sprawling on the rug.

"Get up, Hardy! Get up. This is no time to be lolling about on the carpet! We must sound a Code Red Alert! We must evacuate — we must all get out — now! It's so wonderful!"

"C-Commander, I don't understand," Beef Hardy stammered, pulling himself to his feet. "If the Schnauzers are going to blow up the Space Academy, why is it wonderful news?"

"Because," answered the headmaster, his beady eyes twinkling like raisins, "I'm going to leave the film here."

"The film?"

"Yes, that dreadful, disgraceful film. The film that was about to end my career. Don't you see, Hardy? I'm going to leave it right here. And when the Schnauzers blow up the Academy, the film will blow up with it! No one will ever see it! I'm saved! I'm saved!"

"I guess that *is* good news, sir," Hardy said, dodging out of the way of another fierce slap on the back.

At that moment, Hunk poked his head back into the office. "About my extra credit, sir — ?"

"Not now! Not now!" Dorque screamed.

Hunk's head disappeared from view once again.

"Sound the Code Red Alert!" Commander Dorque ordered. "It's time to evacuate. We must leave — "

"Hold on a moment, sir," Beef Hardy said thoughtfully, raising his hand to stop the Commander. Hardy's steel-gray eyes suddenly lit up like silver Christmas tree ornaments. "I believe I have a good idea, sir. I think you'll like this one."

"Hurry," Dorque said impatiently. "We have to get everyone out before the attack."

"Not everyone," Hardy said, a sly smile forming on his hard, cold face.

"Huh?"

"Well, I was just thinking, sir . . ."

"Yes, Hardy?"

"You're leaving that film behind, right? Well,

why not leave your other problem behind, too?"

"Hardy, you mean — "

Hardy nodded, his face breaking into a full grin. "Yes. Why not leave the four Space Cadets behind, too?"

Commander Dorque had to think it over for only one-tenth of one-tenth of a second. "Yes!" he cried, climbing back up onto his desk to do another jig. "Yes! Excellent, Hardy! Excellent!" His surprisingly little feet tapped happily away until most of the finish was scuffed off the desktop.

"I will tell them it's a special honor," Dorque said happily. "A special patrol for just the four of them. Home Patrol! That's what I'll call it."

"I'm sure they'll be flattered, sir," Hardy said, grinning fiercely.

"Excellent! Excellent! What a happy day! We're going to be destroyed!" Dorque cried jubilantly. "Excellent idea, my boy! Now let's get packed and get out of here!"

"Okay, sir!" Hardy said proudly, giving the Commander a hearty salute and turning to leave.

"And one other thing," Dorque called after him. "Remind me, Hardy, to give you *extra credit* for this idea!"

# 11

"WHAT AN HONOR!" Hunk cheered.

"We are *on patrol!*" Rip exclaimed, slapping Shaky a hard high-five that sprained three of his fingers.

"I knew we'd get extra credit if we did a project," Andy said, his gears whirring excitedly. "But what's a project?"

The four of them were standing in the deserted main lobby, patrolling the front entrance. They stood alertly beside one of the glass doors, their eyes attentively scanning the vast entranceway. There wasn't much to see. There wasn't another living soul within twenty miles.

"Guys, did you see how happy we made Commander Dorque when he assigned us to Home Patrol?" Hunk asked.

"Yes," Shaky agreed, trying to get the feeling back in the hand that Rip had slapped. "He was just so happy that we'd finally come through for him, and he could finally reward us."

"Man, what a day! What a day!" Rip declared happily. He tried to slap Shaky another high-five, but Shaky dived to the floor, and Rip's open hand sailed over his head into thin air. "Let's go on kitchen patrol, guys. All of this responsibility is making me hungry!"

They raced to the kitchen, bumping each other out of the way as they ran. Once inside, they tore through the well-stocked pantry, pulling out turkey legs, ham, whole apple pies, gallon drums of ice cream, gobbling as they explored.

"I think I could get used to having all this responsibility," Rip said with a grin, chocolate ice cream running down his chin.

After a while, they were too stuffed to move. Shaky lay sprawled across one of the long tables, moaning softly to himself. Andy, for some strange reason, had a bottle of olive oil tilted over his mouth and was drinking it down. Hunk sat thinking about Debby Dorque, imagining what a fabulous couple they'd make if only she were as great-looking as he was. Rip continued to eat, stuffing the contents of a bowl of cold mashed potatoes into his open mouth.

"Maybe we should march or something since we're on patrol," Andy suggested, licking his lips as he tossed away the empty olive oil bottle.

Shaky groaned but didn't move from his position on the tabletop. Rip burped. Only a medium burp for him. It lasted less than two minutes.

"No need to march," Hunk said drowsily. "There's no one here. Everyone left, remember?"

He closed his eyes, picturing his affectionate farewell from Debby Dorque. As everyone ran out of the building, heading frantically for the spaceship launching docks, she had hurried up to Hunk.

"I'm so proud of you," she had gushed, throwing her arms around him. "You're so brave! All four of you!"

"I know," he had modestly replied.

"I wish I could stay and be on Home Patrol with you," she had told him. And then she'd added, "It would be so . . . romantic."

"Yes, I know," he had replied, admiring his reflection in her eyes.

"Daddy has been so happy," she had said, shouting over the alarm sirens. "He's been as happy as a little boy ever since you earned the extra credit. I guess he's proud of you, too."

"Yeah, I know," Hunk had said.

And then her father had appeared, ferociously tugging Debby away by the arm, looking very eager to exit the building along with all the others. And Debby had waved and thrown Hunk a kiss, and then disappeared out the doors, the sirens still wailing.

"I don't know why they're so eager to leave," Hunk had said to Rip, shaking his head.

"It's just a space maneuvers drill," Rip had replied. "A stupid drill. We're the lucky ones. We get to stay here and be comfortable."

"Well, we deserve it," Shaky had insisted. "We worked hard for this privilege."

"Yeah," Andy had added, "we're finally getting what we deserve."

As the four Space Cadets moaned quietly in the mess hall, having stuffed themselves into near-coma with their enormous lunch, the Schnauzer war squadron was hurtling through space, less than an hour away.

In the lead spacecraft, their battle leader, General Schnauzerkopf, had his eye on the radar, watching the green-and-blue planet Earth loom larger on the screen. Checking the weaponry, he turned to his second-in-command, Lieutenant Schnauzerlegg.

"Take no prisoners!" the General cried. "Our valuable property has been degraded, and the pride of our nation has been besmirched! We will fight to the last Schnauzer to avenge this heinous insult against our people and all we stand for!"

"Cut the baloney, sir," said the Lieutenant.

"What are we actually going to do when we get to the Space Academy?"

"We're going to massacre everyone we see," replied the General, a cruel smile forming on his crusty lips. "And then we're going to blow the place up real good!"

# 12

"YO — BEING ON HOME PATROL is a real hoot," Hunk said.

"Yeah — especially since there's nothing to patrol," Rip agreed.

"But won't we get into trouble being in here?" Shaky asked, nervously looking back to the door.

They had decided to do what any normal, red-blooded young cadets would do when left all alone in the Space Academy — search the girls' rooms!

"No sweat," Hunk told Shaky. "I told Andy to stand guard outside the door. He'll alert us if they come back early from their space maneuvers drill."

The three happy cadets began gleefully pawing through the dresser drawers, giggling at the lacy things inside.

"Hey — look at this!" Hunk cried. He pulled a photograph out of the bottom drawer. "Look —

it's a picture of Beef Hardy, and it's got lipstick kisses on it!"

Rip and Shaky hurried to look at it over Hunk's shoulder. "Whose room is this, anyway?" Rip asked, making an ugly face at Beef's smiling likeness.

"Cammy Cheesewell's," Shaky said.

"How do you think she got these lip-prints on his picture?" Hunk asked. He couldn't imagine anyone actually kissing something that looked like Beef Hardy.

"Hey — forget the picture. Look at this!" Rip shouted from inside Cammy's clothes closet.

"I don't believe it!" Shaky cried, sticking his head into the closet.

Hunk put the Beef Hardy portrait back in its drawer and hurried over to his startled buddies. They were staring at the pile of cadet uniform pants in Cadet Cheesewell's closet.

"Yo — how did *our pants* get into Cammy Cheesewell's closet?" Hunk wanted to know.

The other two just stared in bewilderment.

"Maybe it's her hobby or something," Shaky said, sifting through the pile and finding his favorite pair of gym shorts. "You know, like a stamp collection. Only she collects pants."

"Weird hobby," Hunk said, scratching his head.

"Well, I guess we can return these to the guys we stole them from," Rip suggested, pointing to the "borrowed" pants they were wearing.

"Yeah. And let's take back our stuff while we have the chance," Hunk said, grabbing up pants and piling them onto his shoulder.

A short while later, the three of them stepped out into the hallway, loaded down with the rescued pants. "Yo — Andy!" Hunk called, not finding him at his post outside the door.

"There he is," Shaky said, pointing.

They hurried down the corridor to an open supply closet, where they found Andy sitting on some large, fifty-pound burlap bags, eating a handful of white powder. "Now *this* is what I wanted to use to sweeten the pea soup," Andy said, taking another handful of the powder and tossing it into his mouth.

Hunk read the stenciled label on the bags: CONCRETE.

"Andy . . . you're eating concrete," he told his friend.

"I know," the android said, his mouth full. "And if I had used this in the first place, we could've gotten extra credit for the soup. Here. Want some?" He held up a handful to his buddies.

They all turned down his generous offer.

"You sure?" Andy urged, disappointed. "It's very filling."

"Really?" Rip said. "Maybe I'll try some."

"Whoa! Stand back! I've got an idea," Hunk cried, pulling back Rip's outstretched hand.

"It doesn't have anything to do with hitting me over a net, does it?" Shaky asked shakily.

"No way," Hunk said enthusiastically, patting his nervous pal on the shoulder. "Listen, guys, we've got nothing much to do on this Home Patrol, right?" They reluctantly agreed. "So let's surprise the Commander when he gets back. Let's do something and get even *more* credit."

"You mean a project?" Andy asked, thick, gooey concrete running down his chin.

"Yes. A project!" Hunk declared. "Let's put our pants away. And then we'll drag that concrete out. Come on, guys. This will be way cool. And if we get even *more* extra credit, maybe Commander Dorque will assign us to Home Patrol again!"


In orbit high above Earth, Commander Dorque settled back in the tall command chair of the Space Patrol cruiser, put his feet up on the console in front of him, and sighed peacefully. Far below, he knew, the Space Academy was being blown to bits by the angry Schnauzers.

What a pity.

Down on Earth, the dreadful, embarrassing film was probably ashes by now.

And the four Space Cadets?

What a pity . . .

Commander Dorque closed his eyes and dreamily snoozed. He hadn't felt this peaceful in ages. Now all he had to do was wait for the all-clear from General Outt. Then he could return to Earth to survey the dreadful damage and then, casting his "sorrow" aside, move on to a new and better assignment.

Dorque was still snoozing peacefully, a big smile on his face, when his daughter Debby burst into the control center with a loud cry of "Daddy!"

Startled awake, the Commander gave a loud snort and fell out of the chair. Debby reached down and pulled him up by the shoulders.

"I told you never to call me Daddy in front of the troops," he scolded, gesturing to the other officers around him who were busily manning the controls.

"Sorry," Debby apologized. "Commander Daddy — "

"That's better." He rearranged himself in the big command chair. When he sat up straight in it, his feet didn't reach the floor.

"When are we going back to the Space Academy?" his daughter demanded. "It's boring up here. All we do is orbit the Earth, orbit the Earth. We're not doing any maneuvers or drills or anything. I want to go home."

"I think orbiting is kind of exciting," Dorque told her. "I don't mind orbiting for a while." Until all of my problems down on Earth are blown to smithereens, he thought pleasantly.

Debby tossed her blonde hair behind her shoulders. "Well, I'm bored, Commander Daddy. I really want to go back to the Academy. I'm worried about Hunk and his friends."

"Oh, I wouldn't worry about them," the Commander said, unable to suppress a grin.

"Well, when *are* we going back?" Debby demanded.

Commander Dorque took a deep breath. He knew he'd have to tell his daughter the truth sooner or later. Any minute now, General Outt would be radioing with the news that the Academy was now a pile of smoldering rubble.

"I might as well tell you," he said, shifting uncomfortably on the big chair. "We're not going back."

"Huh?"

"We're not going back," he repeated. "We're at war. The Schnauzers are on their way right now to blow up the Space Academy."

"But — but that's ridiculous!" Debby cried, her pretty face suddenly distorted by shock and disbelief.

"I know," Commander Dorque said, sighing. "But it's the truth."

"But that's *impossible*!" Debby shrieked. "The Space Patrol will intercept them. The Space Patrol won't let the Schnauzers fly in and destroy our Academy! No way!"

"I'm sorry, my dear daughter, but you're wrong," Commander Dorque said softly. "The

Space Patrol has agreed to let the Schnauzers destroy the Academy. They decided that after what we did to them, it's only fair."

Commander Dorque briefly described what had been done to the Schnauzers' ancient, price-less mural, the reason the war had been declared. His daughter listened impatiently, shaking her head, still not believing this was all happen-ing.

"But — but, Daddy!" she cried in horror, for-getting her father's instructions about how he should be addressed. "Hunk and his friends — they'll all be killed!"

"They'll die heroes," Commander Dorque said, hoping his words were a comfort to her.

They *certainly* were a comfort — to *him*!

The twelve black and gold ships lit up the sky as they descended on the landing pads just beyond the tall Space Academy Tower. Moments later, the Schnauzer attack force, an army of more than two hundred well-trained Schnauzers shouldering automatic laser weapons, emerged from the ships.

Led by General Schnauzerkopf, they marched briskly in three lines, their weapons at the ready. They burst through the front doors and began their thorough search of the building.

Their plan was to destroy anything and anyone who moved.

# 13

HALF AN HOUR LATER, the disappointed Schnauzers were still trudging through the hallways, looking for someone to blast to bits.

"What kind of a battle is this?" Lieutenant Schnauzerlegg whined to the General. "There's no one here. This is too easy."

"So much the better," the General replied, leading the way down another deserted corridor. "When we blow up this building, we'll blow it up clean. Know what I mean?"

"No," the Lieutenant replied. "I haven't the slightest idea of what you're talking about."

"Keep your eyes peeled," General Schnauzerkopf warned.

The Lieutenant's rhinolike face filled with dismay. "Huh? What does *that* mean?!"

They stopped in front of Commander Dorque's closed office door. Just for fun, General Schnauzerkopf kicked the door down.

Playing it safe, the members of the General's

squad raised their weapons before entering the office. But it was as empty as every other room in the building.

They were about to leave when the General spotted the movie projector in the back of the room. "Hey — a movie!" he exclaimed excitedly. "Cut the lights, Lieutenant. Let's take a look at it. There's nothing else of much interest here, after all. Maybe it will give us some clues as to where Commander Dorque and his cadets have escaped to."

The General took a seat in Commander Dorque's leather chair. His soldiers squeezed into the office and, leaning on their weapons, sat down cross-legged on the carpet. A few minutes later, the projector had been rewound and the beginning of the film was flickering onto the screen.

Had he been able to witness this scene, Commander Dorque would have been embarrassed all over again. For there he was on the screen, falling into the deep pile of fertilizer, scrambling around in it until he was swimming in the muck.

The Schnauzer General roared with laughter, as did his men. The entire office quaked as they laughed until crocodile tears poured down their rhinoceros faces.

They thought this was hilarious.

They found the pea soup scene even more hilarious.

They roared and slapped their knees as the cadets heaved up their green lunches. General Schnauzerkopf laughed so hard, the medals popped off his uniform jacket.

And as the volleyball tournament began and the four Space Cadets appeared in their ridiculous, polka dot boxer shorts, the Schnauzers went completely out of control, laughing until they couldn't breathe, choking on their own laughter.

Several minutes later, when the film had run to the end and was whipping around its spool, and the soldiers had finally caught their breaths and managed to stop bellowing with laughter, the Schnauzer General rose to his feet and stepped to the front of the room.

"Gentlemen," he said, pacing as he addressed them in a loud, authoritative voice. "Gentlemen, this Academy has to be the stupidest place on Earth."

The men all cheered and shouted out their agreement.

"The cadets appear to be nincompoops," the General continued, using very strong language for a Schnauzer. "And their leader appears to be the biggest nincompoop of all!"

Once again the men all cheered and shouted out their agreement.

"We cannot attack this place," the General announced.

A silence fell on the room as the soldiers' faces revealed their surprise.

"We cannot attack this place because we would be insulting ourselves to fight such an unworthy opponent," General Schnauzerkopf continued. "Great soldiers fight great opponents. We would only degrade and humiliate ourselves by wasting our energies on these . . . these . . ."

Words failed the General. He turned and headed toward the doorway, still shaking his head.

"Pack up," the Lieutenant commanded the men. "Let's get out of here as fast as we can. Maybe our attack won't get in the newspapers and embarrass us."

The soldiers quickly climbed to their feet. Several of them grumbled quietly, disappointed that they didn't get to wipe the building away.

"Oh, and bring that movie," ordered the General from the doorway. "I want to see it again when we get home. It's an absolute laugh riot. I give it two thumbs up!"

He held up his right hand, which had two thumbs on it.

Still chuckling, he led the way back to the sleek battle spaceships. A few minutes later, the Schnauzers blasted off, heading back to their planet, leaving the Space Academy gleaming red and gold in the late afternoon sun.

*　*　*

In back, where they were working hard under the still-sweltering sun, Hunk and his three companions put down their trowels and gazed up at the sky as the spaceships took off, momentarily covering the sun in flames of their own, and thick clouds of gray exhaust smoke.

"Wonder who that was," Hunk said, wiping the sweat off his handsome forehead with the back of his concrete-splotched hand.

"Yeah. I saw them land a while ago," Shaky said.

"Couldn't have been important," Rip added. "Or they would've hung around."

"They were probably lost," Andy suggested. Then he beeped and gave the time.

"Hey — it's getting late, guys," Hunk said, picking up his trowel. "Back to work."

Two hundred miles up in space, the Space Patrol cruisers still orbited Earth. When Debby Dorque returned to the control center a few hours after her first visit, she found her father with his head down on the console, whimpering noisily, fat tears rolling down his cheeks.

"Daddy — " Debby gasped. "Bad news? From back home?" Her face went white. She began to tremble all over, expecting the worst.

"Yes," Commander Dorque managed to say in

a weak, trembling voice. "News from back home. I just heard from General Outt."

"Ohh." Debby sighed, her voice catching in her throat. "Don't tell me — "

"Everything is okay," Commander Dorque whimpered sadly. "The Schnauzers attacked, but were driven away. There is no damage to the building. No damage to . . . anyone." He tried to say more, but was overcome by emotion and burst into loud, heartbreaking sobs.

"Then it's good news?" Debby cried, stunned. "It's good news? Hunk is okay? Everyone is okay?"

Commander Dorque, weeping hard, could only nod.

"Daddy — if it's good news . . . if Hunk and his friends are okay . . . why are you crying like that?"

"Oh." Commander Dorque pulled himself upright. "These are . . . uh . . . tears of *joy,*" he explained.

# 14

"Hunk! You're okay!" Debby Dorque cried jubilantly. She ran across the Space Academy landing field and threw her arms around him. "You're okay!"

"Yeah. Fine," he said casually, surprised by the emotional welcome. "I over-ate a little. You know. Gave me gas. But I'm okay."

"Oh, you're so modest!" she gushed.

"Me?" He wondered if she'd gone space crazy up in orbit. What was her problem, anyway?

Debby proceeded to hug the other three Space Cadets joyfully, telling them each how brave they were. They were as confused as Hunk. They really hadn't done much, after all.

A short while later, Commander Dorque droopily trudged across the field and approached them. He gave a weary salute and kept walking.

"Daddy — aren't you going to *say* anything to them?" his daughter scolded.

Commander Dorque grudgingly stopped and

turned around. "How did you guys do it?" he muttered.

"Huh? Do what?" Hunk asked.

"You know. Fend off the Schnauzers," he said impatiently.

"Schnauzers?" Hunk replied. "Were there Schnauzers here?"

"Hunk is being modest," Debby told her father. "All four of them are just so modest!" She squealed and gave Hunk a hug around the waist. "You're a hero!"

Commander Dorque made a sour face.

Hunk and his three buddies looked very confused. Then Hunk suddenly remembered he had something to show the Commander. "Uh . . . sir?"

Dorque groaned unhappily. All he could think of was getting inside and taking a warm bath. And not coming out for maybe two or three years. "What is it?" he snapped.

"Well, my pals and I did a little something while you were away. A little project, you might say," Hunk began.

"Yeah. We want to get more extra credit," Rip added, grinning.

*More* extra credit? thought the unhappy Commander. What *more* can they do? They've already singlehandedly driven away one of the toughest armies in the galaxy!

"Please — follow us," Hunk pleaded. A smile

crossed his handsome face. "I think you'll be very pleased at what we've done."

"Some other time," Commander Dorque snarled.

"Come on, Daddy. Do it right now," Debby scolded. "You *owe* them."

"Oh, space spit!" Dorque grumbled, but he reluctantly allowed Debby to pull him along as they followed Hunk and his friends.

Hunk led them across the Rifle Practice Field to the small, rectangular field to the left of it. "There it is!" he proclaimed proudly, and pointed to the enormous, flat concrete slab stretching out over the entire field.

Commander Dorque's mouth dropped open and he gaped in shock and horror. "What — what — what — what — ?"

"We built it ourselves on this empty field," Shaky said proudly.

"What — what — what — ?" the stunned Commander repeated, his eyes bulging out of his now-crimson face.

"It's a skating rink," Hunk explained proudly. "You know. For roller-skating. Everyone can use it."

"But — my sweet — my sweet — my prize sweet potatoes!" Commander Dorque cried.

"Yeah. There *were* a lot of weeds we had to pull out before we poured the concrete," Hunk said.

Commander Dorque uttered a low wail. He trembled all over and then toppled to his quivering knees.

My sweet potatoes, he thought. My prize sweet potatoes. The sweetest, rarest, chewiest sweet potatoes in the galaxy. Buried under a slab of concrete.

And now that idiot Hunk was grinning at him expectantly, explaining how they got the concrete so smooth.

My sweet potatoes. Gone. Gone. Gone forever.

"So we hope you'll consider giving us extra credit," Hunk was saying, grinning at the Commander's daughter, who grinned back at him warmly.

Extra credit?? Dorque thought, feeling the rage course through his body.

I'll *kill* him! I'll kill all four of them!

No. He realized he couldn't do that. General Outt was on his way at that very moment bringing Heroes' Medals for them. They were going to be on TV. A parade was being planned in their honor.

The Commander stared at the ugly slab of concrete. How did they *do* it? he asked himself. How did they fight off an entire army *and* find the time to plow under my precious sweet potato crop and bury them under all that concrete?

It was too much for him. His brain seemed to explode. He swooned and toppled face forward.

Into the pile of fertilizer.

A camera crew that had just arrived to interview the four Space Cadet heroes whirred into action, capturing the moment as the Commander flopped about in the syrupy slime, struggling to stand up.

Smiling proudly at Hunk, Debby Dorque took his arm and quietly led him away from the frantic scene. Behind them, Rip was bending over the floundering Commander. "So what's your decision on the extra credit?" they could hear Rip ask.

They couldn't hear the Commander's reply.

But they kept on walking anyway.

## About the Author

R.L. STINE has been a Space Cadet his entire life. He is also the author of more than one hundred books of humor, adventure, horror, and mystery for young readers. In addition to his publishing work, he is head writer of the children's TV show *Eureeka's Castle*.

Bob lives in New York City with his wife, Jane, and their son, Matt.

**APPLE** PAPERBACKS

IT'S FAR OUT!

IT'S TOTALLY RIDICULOUS...

# IT'S THE
# WILD AND CRAZY
# ADVENTURE SERIES:

# SPACE
# CADETS

## By R.L. Stine

Meet the funniest, most idiotic, most inept cadets in the history of the Space Academy....NASA was never like this!

☐ BAH44745-9   #1 **Jerks-in-Training**        $2.75
☐ BAH44746-7   #2 **Losers in Space**          $2.75
☐ BAH44747-5   #3 **Bozos on Patrol**          $2.75

**Available wherever you buy books, or use this order form.**

Scholastic Inc., P.O. Box 7502, 2931 East McCarty Street, Jefferson City, MO 65102

Please send me the books I have checked above. I am enclosing $_____ (please add $2.00 to cover shipping and handling). Send check or money order -- no cash or C.O.D.s please.

Name _____

Address _____

City _____ State/Zip _____

Please allow four to six weeks for delivery. Offer good in the U.S. only. Sorry, mail orders are not available to residents of Canada. Prices subject to change.

SC991